GOING UP

AMANDA RADLEY

Sign Up to Win

Firstly, thank you for purchasing *Going Up* I really appreciate your support and hope you enjoy the book!

Head over to my website and sign up to my mailing list to be kept up to date with all my latest releases, promotions, and giveaways.

www.amandaradley.com

GOING UP

The Suited Idiot

JONATHAN ADDINGTON LEANED BACK IN HIS CHAIR. His fingers were interlaced behind his head, and a slimy grin slithered across his young features. Selina wondered how he ever managed to do business with anyone with an expression and attitude like that. He probably thought he was charming, roguish. In truth, his unpleasantness was too strong to be covered by a half-hearted grin.

"So, you see what I'm saying?"

He'd said a lot since he entered Selina's office ten minutes ago. Most of it was focused on the end-of-year figures and the predicted turnover for the coming period. Namely, the fact that profits were down.

Of course, he'd started by mentioning how Selina's hard work over the years had saved the company from bankruptcy, but that was only a pathetic attempt to butter her up before diving into a conversation about how revenues continued to drop.

"You're saying," Selina said, leaning into her high back

chair and pinning him with a look, "that you want further cuts."

"Exactly." Jonathan sat forward. He brought his hand up and made a scissor action with his fingers. "Chop, chop. I thought you might have some ideas?"

It took every single piece of willpower that Selina possessed to not roll her eyes at him. She placed her hands on her desk and gently rolled her chair back. She stood up and walked over to the large office window, which, on the twelfth floor, overlooked the gloomy car park and railway line.

Not the office on the thirteenth floor that overlooked the award-winning park, the one she had been coveting for nearly thirty years.

While many people would have been happy as operations director for a top accountancy firm, Selina Hale wasn't. She'd been eyeing promotion to the board since the day she walked into the offices of Nicholas Addington and Sons.

The thirteenth floor was the prize. The lifelong goal. Selina was driven solely by her desire to become a member of the board, where she could finally make some dramatic changes to the company and receive the benefits of such transformations by way of hefty dividends.

She was well paid for her current role, of course, but she found it grating that she was constantly the one developing and implementing changes that kept the business afloat, only to receive a standard salary. Meanwhile, the shareholders were living a life of luxury and benefitting from her hard work.

Selina craved the status, the power, the respect, and the money. And she had it all within her grasp.

Jonathan, however, was useless. Only in his role because his father owned the company, he was a board member with no real power. Despite an expensive education in a Scandinavian business school, Jonathan had no head for corporate dealings. He wanted to prove himself worthy of his father's legacy and eventually take over the firm, but he was sensible enough to understand that he couldn't do it alone and sought assistance wherever he could find it.

It hadn't taken Selina long to get Jonathan onside and make him reliant on *her* for that advice. She wasn't foolish enough to just give him the advice. No, she wanted to do the work, even when the work was restructuring the business and making scores of people redundant.

Because being willing to do the dirty work was how people got noticed.

"I've also been looking at the predictions," Selina said, looking out of the window at some garbage beside the railway tracks. "Of course, if I'd not implemented my previous round of cost-saving initiatives, we'd be in a much worse state."

She turned around and folded her arms, not allowing him to reply before she continued. "The marketing team is ripe for a little fat-cutting. Margaret doesn't seem to feel the pinch like the rest of us, if her team breakfast meetings in the boardroom are anything to go by. And I know we're all supposed to be tweeting and liking everything with a pulse, but there is no place for that in an accountancy firm. Devonshire Estates are not going to hire us to restructure their taxes because of a quirky video explaining what VAT is."

She walked back to her desk and opened the top drawer, studying the folder she pulled out before handing it to him.

"My recommendations. They lose half their team, and social media is stripped back to interns. It's for children, so children might as well run it. I wouldn't want us to appear out of touch by not having any online presence, of course. It's not the Stone Age."

Jonathan opened the folder and flipped through the scant details it contained. She wasn't about to give away all of her plans, just the headline facts and figures.

"As you can see, I recommend a substantial cut of their budget. When they can prove that they are making more than they are spending, they may apply to have it back. But at the moment, I'm not seeing much proof that the marketing budget is being spent effectively."

Selina sat down and waited for Jonathan to read through the small pack.

He skimmed it, at best, before closing the folder and placing it back on her desk. "Ten steps ahead as always, Selina."

She smiled and spread her hands. "That's what I'm here for. Are you happy for me to implement the plan?"

He nodded eagerly. "Go ahead."

She knew he was happy to be saving money and relieved that it would be Selina doing the deed. That allowed Jonathan to save face and walk around the office looking forlorn and pretending it had nothing to do with him.

It was the perfect arrangement. Jonathan would still be well liked by the staff. Selina would implement the next round of operational tweaks that would stabilise the business financials. And get her noticed by the board.

"Speaking of marketing," Jonathan added, "did you see the cost for the new website?"

This time Selina did roll her eyes.

"I did," she confirmed. "I've already looked into alternative suppliers. This is just another example of Margaret overspending. How hard can it be to build a website? That quote was obscene."

Jonathan smiled and stood up. "I knew you'd have it all in hand."

"You can rely on me," she told him. "I'll have new proposal documents to you for the website by early next week. And I can assure you, we won't have to sell organs to fund it."

"Fantastic." He tapped his watch. "I have to get going. Drop me an email if you need anything."

More golf, she assumed. Jonathan spent more time networking on the green than he did in his office, which suited Selina perfectly. He asked for solutions to problems she already knew existed. She provided the solutions and implemented them with his blessing. While he was on the golf course, the entire board were informed of her ongoing progress, and her place on the thirteenth floor moved a step closer. Sometimes it felt too easy.

"I will. Enjoy your afternoon."

She smiled in farewell and watched him leave her glass-walled haven. He strolled through the outer office like a man without a care in the world. She supposed that was exactly what he was. He'd never had to do a real day's work in his life.

As soon as he left, Gemma walked into the office.

Well, more like waddled. Selina regarded Gemma's pregnancy bulge and let out a small sigh. Gemma was one of the few assistants she had managed to train to become acceptable, and now the foolish redhead had decided to start a family with her new husband.

"Your solicitor called and would like you to call him back when you have time," Gemma said. "And Mark from IT says he can't do tomorrow morning anymore but wonders if you're free at two on Friday."

"Am I?" Selina asked disinterestedly. She didn't pay an assistant so she could waste her time committing her own schedule to memory.

"You are. You have a meeting with Margaret at one, but you scheduled it in for an hour."

Selina paused, staring into space for a moment while she mentally calculated if she'd need longer to tell Margaret that her team and budget were being reduced by seventy-five percent.

"That should be fine," Selina replied. Margaret would complain and rant for a while, but she was stick thin and training for the London Marathon so would no doubt run out of energy before the hour was up.

Gemma shifted from foot to foot with discomfort. Her pregnancy had made her balloon, to the extent that Selina wasn't entirely sure her assistant was growing a human baby. From the size of her, there were good odds it was an elephant calf.

"I'll have a latte from Edge." Selina picked up her

mobile and scrolled through her address book to find her solicitor.

She noticed Gemma's lack of enthusiasm at going out for coffee, but she wasn't about to start drinking the swill from the staff room. It really wasn't Selina's fault that Gemma could no longer see her ankles.

"Problem?"

"No, Selina," her assistant answered quickly. "Just a latte? Would you like something to eat for later?"

And save you from having to do two visits? Selina thought to herself. *No, thank you.*

"No. Just the latte." Selina turned in her chair, indicating that the conversation was over. She didn't need to turn to hear Gemma plod out of the office.

Gemma's productivity since pregnancy had taken a nosedive. Maternity leave was still a way off, and Selina didn't know if Gemma was even planning on coming back. The notion of sacking her and getting an agency worker was tempting, but she was hardly on the human resources department's Christmas card list as it was. Sacking her pregnant assistant before she went on maternity would probably not endear her to anyone.

Selina took a deep breath and pressed Jeremy's name. She placed the phone to her ear and listened to the dial tone, feeling more stressed with each one she heard.

"Ah, she lives," her solicitor answered. "I wasn't sure, as you've been ignoring my calls for two days."

"I'm extremely busy, Jeremy." Half true. Although, she'd find things to do if it meant avoiding this conversation.

"Well, your tactical avoidance of matters has landed us with a demand."

"English, Jeremy?"

"Your wife—"

"Ex-wife," Selina corrected.

"Not yet. Your wife's solicitor has sent a letter saying that if a reasonable settlement is not met soon, then you will be going to court. To allow a judge to distribute assets and finalise the divorce."

"Precisely what I want to happen," Selina said.

"Selina, we have spoken about this. Court is a bad idea."

"So you keep saying, but I think attending court and explaining the whole situation to a judge will ensure not a single penny of my money gets into the hands of that conniving bitch."

Jeremy let out a heartfelt sigh. "Selina…"

"When's the date?" she asked. She was already planning a few choice statements she'd enjoy making.

"Selina," Jeremy said, more forcefully this time. "You hired me to advise you. I strongly advise against going to court. To be frank, your reputation and personality are not going to do you any favours."

"My personality?" Selina spluttered.

"There's a high likelihood that the court will rule in your wife's favour after spending a few minutes in your company."

"Well, that's uncalled for. I thought you were on my side."

"I am. Which is why I'm telling you that you come across rather harsh on a good day. When you're cross, you're like a steamroller with anger management issues. Courts are quiet, calm places that like to distribute judgement in a fair and reasonable manner. You will not do well there."

Selina got to her feet and walked over to the window. She looked down and could see Gemma slowly making her way across the car park to the closest coffee shop, Edge.

"I'm not meeting with her," Selina argued.

"I know, but you can't ignore every communication from her solicitor either. If you continue to do that, then court will be her only option. And I cannot stress enough—"

"They'll hate me, I get it." Selina let out a sigh. She frowned and leaned closer to the window. She blinked, her eyes not quite believing what they saw.

There was a homeless person living in the car park.

It was hard to tell from her office, but they seemed to be wrapped in a sleeping bag, in plain sight of any clients who could be using the car park. Of course, Gemma stopped and gave them some money.

"Idiot," Selina muttered. Gemma should be using her brain and calling someone to remove the homeless person, not giving them money and encouraging them to stay and clutter up the area.

"Pardon?" Jeremy asked.

"Not you. I'm going to have to call you back."

"Selina—"

She hung up the call and quickly rang John in the facilities department, her eyes fixed on the car park's new inhabitant.

"Facilities," John gruffly answered.

"There's a vagrant in the car park," Selina said.

"The one to the rear?" John asked.

"No, the one three miles away that I can miraculously see from my window which overlooks the rear car park." Selina glanced up at the ceiling and shook her head. She couldn't believe the level of incompetence at this company. "Get security out there and move them on."

"We can't do that. It's a public car park which we rent spaces in. We don't own it. We'd have to get the police to move them on, and the police usually have better things to do than respond to those calls."

"Call the police then," she insisted. "It doesn't look good for our clients to be parking their car next to some criminal. I'd think that's quite obvious, John. Isn't it?"

There was a slight pause, probably while John debated if it was worth arguing with the operations director just two years out from his retirement.

"I'll give them a ring," he replied neutrally.

Selina hung up the call. She folded her arms and glared down at the scene below. Cars meandered around looking for an empty space, while her assistant meandered even more slowly on her way to Edge. Selina's latte would no doubt be frozen by the time it got to her. And a nomad clad in a likely smelly sleeping bag sat in plain sight of everyone.

Promotion to the thirteenth floor couldn't come soon enough.

2

An Empty Office

SELINA TUCKED HER FOLDER UNDER HER ARM AND hurried out of the meeting room. She couldn't believe the nerve of some people. Bloody Margaret had commandeered what should have been a thirty-minute meeting about office supplies. She'd had to suffer through an hour and a half talking about a client appreciation event she wasn't entirely sure would bring in the revenues that Margaret claimed.

Ordinarily she would have shut the whole thing down and got the discussion back on track, but when the chairman of the board, Nicholas Addington, seemed interested in the conversation, she had found that she was stuck. Trying to reroute the conversation to office supplies was impossible once Margaret started to discuss the wine list for the event.

She turned into the main office on the twelfth floor and was disappointed, but not surprised, to see row upon row of empty desks. It was five-thirty, and it seemed that not a single person was interested in staying late to ensure the company's survival.

She crossed the floor quickly and approached her corner office. A glance at Gemma's desk confirmed her suspicions that the girl had already left for the day.

Selina rolled her eyes.

She wondered if it was worth doing a time-cost analysis of Gemma's work. While she was undoubtedly more competent than many of Selina's past assistants, at least the less capable ones had worked longer hours. Gemma seemed to value time at home with her husband more than her job.

Gemma was smart in some ways but useless in others. Her inability to see the redundancies and belt-tightening around her surprised Selina. Unless, she considered, the foolish girl thought that her boss would protect her from the chop.

Selina snorted to herself. If Gemma thought that, then she was more delusional than Selina first thought.

She entered her office and dropped the folder on her desk. Under her keyboard were a couple of handwritten notes. She deposited one regarding a call back from Jeremy straight in the bin and reviewed another with a message from her sister.

Selina blew out a breath and sat down. Her sister had long since given up trying to contact her directly and had started feeding detailed messages through her assistants. This meant that Selina was rarely able to say she didn't get a message without making it seem like her office was shoddily run.

She read the note. Apparently one of her nephews

was having a birthday party, and she was invited. An involuntary shiver run up her spine. A child's birthday celebration wasn't her idea of a fun afternoon. Why she couldn't just send some money in a card, she didn't know.

She leaned back and contemplated which of the two it could be, Peter or Phillip. She cursed her sister for giving her boys the same first initial. How was she supposed to tell them apart?

She flipped back through some pages in her desk planner to remember the last time she'd seen them. After a while she found the day of the dinner party. Six months ago.

Selina slumped in her chair. It was probably time she paid her dues and attended the family gathering.

Her laptop screen was cluttered with pop-up reminders, and she could see her email account was yet again out of control. She pulled the laptop closer and instinctively reached for her coffee mug. Of course, it was empty.

She put it back down again and considered her options.

A quick trip to the staff room or a walk to Edge. A look at her watch, and she conducted a quick mental calculation of how late she'd be working. A trip to Edge to get coffee and a salad for dinner was undoubtedly the best option.

Of course, if her assistant was any good at her job she'd still be in the office and Selina would be able to send her to get it. She picked up a pen and snatched up a Post-It note. She jotted down Gemma's name and then a question mark to remind herself to think about her assistant's future.

Pregnant or not, she was becoming laxer than Selina could tolerate.

Selina grabbed her phone and purse and headed out of the office.

3

Invisible

KATE PUT DOWN HER PENCIL AND STARTED TO clench and unclench her hand. Once the sun went down behind the office block, the cold really started to set in. She had a few more hours before the shelter opened, and she knew from experience that staying put in her current location was her best bet.

Drawing killed the time, and there was a lot of time to kill. She wasn't any good at it and didn't expect to be discovered by some gallery owner, but at least it kept her occupied. The alternative was to sit and stare at passers-by.

She'd discovered very quickly that once you were homeless, you were invisible. There was something about sitting on the street that made you instantly lose your membership to the human race.

The occasional good soul would make eye contact. Sometimes they would smile or nod, but on the whole people would do all they could to avoid you.

It was soul-destroying to find yourself—through no fault of your own—homeless and an outsider.

And so, Kate drew. Scribbles and sketches on scraps of paper that the shelter managed to find for her. Anything to get through the long hours when the shelter was closed during the day.

She heard the sound of heels tapping on the pavement. Glancing up, she saw a businesswoman in a trouser suit marching her way across the car park.

The term 'all business' could have been created specifically for her.

Short, grey hair was swept back, away from her face. She was older but not old enough to have naturally greyed to such an extent. Kate guessed it had been dyed at the first sign of aging. It was a clever strategy and made it very difficult to pin an age on some women.

The businesswoman walked with confidence, more a strut than a walk. Kate imagined that the sound of her approach would strike fear into the hearts of her co-workers.

And, of course, she was on her mobile phone, having a loud conversation without a care for anyone else. Not that there was anyone else to hear it, just Kate and the Robo-Woman crossing the car park like she owned it.

"Why I have to go there and talk to her snivelling little runts, I don't know!" the woman was saying loudly. "I don't even remember which of my two *darling* nephews is having a birthday. So, I suppose I'll be expected to look that up. As if I have the time. I didn't choose to be an aunt. Ghastly business."

Kate stared at the ground in order to avoid eye contact. She didn't like to judge people based on their appearance, but it seemed in this case she was spot on.

Kate remembered family birthday parties, especially those with children. The cake, the balloons, the presents wrapped up in colourful paper. It all seemed so far away now, as if it were a memory from a television programme she had once seen rather than recollections of her own life.

She snatched up the pencil and rummaged through her bag for a fresh piece of sketch paper. She found an envelope containing a letter from the council. A smirk curled at her mouth. Another meeting with her social worker. Another day where she was told that she wasn't in immediate danger and that they therefore wouldn't be able to offer her any assistance.

She sighed. Technically, they were right. She'd seen the desperate people on the streets who needed help much more than she did. People addicted to drugs, people turning to prostitution.

A shiver ran up her spine.

Things weren't that bad for her. She had just enough money to survive through her benefits, and the shelter kept her warm and clean during the hours it was open. And, despite the rude businesswomen, the car park wasn't a bad place to spend her days. It was safe, a lot safer than some of the usual places where homeless people based themselves.

But she hoped one day soon she would finally be moved up the social worker's priority queue and be allocated some kind of housing.

She was trying not to count, but she knew it was coming up to twelve months of being on the streets.

A whole year of her life wasted.

She sniffed and sat up a little straighter.

No, not wasted, she told herself. *Just… different. And this will end. It will.*

She started to sketch on the back of the envelope from the council. The figure of a businesswoman with lasers shooting from her eyes came to her quickly.

No matter how bad things were for her, at least she had a heart. She'd remember the names of any nieces or nephews she had. She'd remember their birthdays and buy them gifts they'd appreciate.

She could hear heels on concrete again. Without even looking up, she knew the woman was back, clearly having visited the coffee shop.

Kate kept her head down and added some little people at the feet of the laser-eyed businesswoman she was drawing. They were running for their lives.

"I told them flat out that I don't care," the woman said, still on the phone. "Just do what I paid you to do and get out of my line of vision. Tradespeople. Honestly."

The woman paused for a moment in front of Kate.

Kate held her breath, wondering what was about to happen. At that moment she'd quite like to be invisible.

She looked up at the same moment a takeaway mug from the coffee shop was placed on the ground. The woman didn't even look at her before she continued walking.

"Well, the kitchen needed to be done. It had been three years. Was I supposed to be looking at stainless steel for the rest of the year? I told them, if that marble sink isn't installed by Friday, then don't come back on Monday. And don't you dare invoice me either."

Kate stared at the drink. She lifted her head and watched the woman walking away.

How dare she! Kate fumed. *She can't even be bothered to look at me. Or say something. Just… dropping off a drink. To make herself feel better. Make her think that she's a decent human being when she clearly isn't.*

Kate grabbed the drink and held it up.

"No, thank you," she called out loudly.

The woman stopped walking. She slowly turned around, a confused look on her face. A paper bag of food and a second takeaway mug were clutched in her free hand.

Kate gestured the cup up towards her, eager for her to return and take it back.

"It's free," the woman explained.

"I don't want it."

The woman paused for a few moments.

"I'll have to call you back, Janine," she said before hanging up her call. She approached and looked down at Kate with barely hidden disdain. "You should probably learn to accept charity, considering your situation."

"I don't need to accept charity from someone who can't remember the names of her nephews and calls them 'snivelling little runts.'"

"How dare you eavesdrop on my conver—"

"Eavesdrop? You were shouting. And I don't want your charity. It's not for me, it's for you."

The woman stared at Kate in shock before spinning on her heel and walking away. Kate lowered the cup. She debated whether she should drink it or throw it away. She took a tentative sniff.

Coffee. Probably not poisoned. But who knows?

Deciding there was no sense in wasting the drink, she took a tentative sip. The burst of bitter flavour danced across her mouth. It had been a while since she'd had a good barista-made cup of coffee. Tasteless instant powder at the shelter was all she had these days, with as much sugar as she could stomach to mask the taste and keep hunger at bay.

Maybe it had been rude to not accept the drink at first, but she'd do so again in an instant. Kate may have been homeless, but she was proud that she hadn't lost her sense of self. She was still Kate Morgan.

When she'd lost everything, she was quick to realise that personal possessions flowed away with considerable ease. But her thoughts, feelings, personality traits, and actions were her own and could never be taken away.

Even if that sometimes meant pride caused her loss. She'd rather not have something than accept a gift from someone she couldn't stand.

4

Not Accustomed to Losing

"Come on, you ridiculous old biddy," Selina mumbled.

She tapped her fingers on the steering wheel of her Porsche as the hundred-year-old woman slowly walked across the road. The lights had changed to green, the sun was rising higher in the sky, but the centenarian wasn't going to let that hurry her along. Clearly, *she* didn't need to get to work.

Selina looked at her wristwatch and let out a sigh. She'd already been delayed by the ambulance on the main road into Parbrook. When the firm made the decision to move to a commuter town outside of London, the theory had been that rent would be cheaper and the surrounding area would be quieter.

Parbrook was certainly cheaper than the central London office they'd had, but the town was a popular residential area with little understanding that busy people had places to be. Selina had also moved her life from a more central location in London to Parbrook. Her commute to work should have been the simplest thing in the world. Except for the local residents and their dawdling.

Selina pressed the palm of her hand into the middle of the steering wheel, and the horn loudly sounded. She intermittently pressed the button, creating a little tune as she sang "hurry up" under her breath.

Finally, the old woman's big toe crossed onto the pavement. Selina put her foot down and sped away from the crossing.

She shook her head. Today was already shaping up to be a bad day. The kitchen fitter had left her without a working sink and now refused to return her calls. The dry cleaner hadn't noticed a missing button on her jacket, so a last-minute change of outfit had been in order. And now she was running late.

She turned into the car park behind the office building and stopped the car in the middle of the road.

"You," she whispered venomously.

She narrowed her eyes and stared at the homeless woman who appeared to be setting up her sleeping bag in the exact location as the day before.

"Don't get too comfy," she muttered.

She drove farther into the car park, into her designated space by the back door to the building.

Yesterday afternoon she had been content to let John handle the matter of the woman in the car park, but now she would deal with it herself.

She was still bitter that the ridiculous woman had the gall to refuse a free hot drink, not to mention had eavesdropped on her conversation.

"Rude, that's what she is," Selina mumbled to herself.

She gathered her belongings and threw them into her bag. "Probably unhinged. Needs to go."

She looked up as Margaret parked next to her.

"Oh, great." Selina pretended to rummage through her bag so that she wouldn't have to walk into the office with the loathsome woman.

Idiots inside the office; rude, ungrateful vagrants outside the office, she thought.

When the barista had messed up her order the night before, and given her both drinks by way of apology, she hadn't known what to do with the second beverage. Handing it to the homeless woman seemed easier than crossing the street to the public bin. Or carrying it up to the office.

But then it was declined, for reasons Selina couldn't begin to fathom or care about.

All that mattered was that the woman needed to go. She was cluttering up the car park and making a bad impression on any clients coming to see them. John seemed to think it wouldn't be an easy task, but Selina was now more determined than ever to get rid of the woman.

"Ungrateful…"

Suddenly, an idea hit her.

Selina was upset by her lack of gratitude, so why not do something that would force the woman to be grateful? A *thank you* could probably be squeezed out of her with the right application of force.

She picked up her phone and rolled it over in her hand a few times while she considered the matter. It didn't take long before a scenario formed in her head and she was calling the manager of Edge.

"Edge Coffee Bar, how may I help?"

"Julian, it's Selina Hale from Addington's."

There was a pregnant pause while Julian presumably panicked about a forgotten order, or worse, another renegotiation of their pricing matrix. Edge provided catering to all of Addington's meetings, and Selina had often sought to cut the budget where necessary. At the end of the day, she signed off on the invoices and Julian knew that. Which meant that Julian owed her a favour.

"O-oh… Hi!" Julian finally found his tongue. "Is there a problem?"

"Yes. One which I already have a marvellous solution to," Selina said. "When I was in the shop the other day, I noticed a board talking about your work in the community."

"Yes?"

"Well, good news, Julian. I have an excellent way for you to help the community, as in me, right now." She gathered her belongings and exited the car. "In the car park of my building is a delightful woman who has fallen through the cracks of society and is tragically homeless."

The security guard quickly opened the door for her, and she swept through without even looking at him. She crossed to the lifts and stabbed the call button.

"Obviously, there is a result here that can suit all of us. You can employ her. Well, I say employ. You can charitably allow her to work for you and gain experience. Then she's no longer out on the street and you have an extra pair of hands. Isn't that just wonderful all round?"

"H-homeless woman?" Julian stammered.

"Yes, you'll see her right away. Sleeping bag, blonde

hair. She's a delight. And just think of how good you'll feel knowing that you saved her from a life of crime and drugs." Selina stabbed the button a few more times. "I'm in the middle of reviewing our catering options, and it would be so lovely to just leave things the way they are. Easier for you, easier for me. But I have to think about perception. If you say you help in the community, then I need to be sure that you really do, and it isn't all marketing messaging with no backbone."

"But... I don't know who she even is—"

"Then you'll talk to her, Julian. Honestly, I can't do everything for you. She's perfectly lovely. I expect you'll want to head out there and offer her some kind of apprenticeship or something. Rather soon."

She hung up the call and stepped into the elevator. She stared longingly at the button for the top floor for a few moments. She even lifted her hand and traced the digits of the thirteenth-floor button, but then she quickly pulled her hand away and stabbed at the twelve instead.

By the time Selina had entered her office a few minutes later, she could see the homeless woman speaking with Julian in the car park below. She waited by the window, watching the encounter. She was too far away to see in any detail, but she was satisfied that her plan had worked when the woman started to gather up her sleeping bag and belongings and followed Julian towards Edge.

"Excellent," she said to herself.

She made a mental note to pop into Edge that evening and extract an apology and a thank you from the woman.

5

Becoming Visible

Kate walked around the trendy coffee shop, taking it all in. It was all distressed wood, bare walls, and metal rails. In one corner was a cluster of leather tub chairs holding a group of mums with babies.

"They come in twice a week," Julian explained. "We have a calm vibe, so the mothers like that."

"I bet," Kate agreed.

She still wasn't quite sure about Julian or his intentions. She'd been on the streets for a while, and no local business owner had ever walked up to her and offered her a position before.

He'd been quite clear that it would be a temporary trial; she'd work for free in return for three meals a day. After a week or so, they'd review.

It sounded like a dream come true.

Which was why Kate was wary.

She'd not experienced much good luck in her life, but she wasn't about to refuse a potential life-saving offer such as this.

She'd do her best, work as hard as she could, and try to earn employment, while keeping an eagle eye on what was happening around her. Stories of people being snatched off the street and sold into human slavery rang in her ears.

"I'll need some details from you, for the insurance," Julian said. "If you want to come through to the office?"

Kate looked at the two staff members working behind the counter. They seemed happy and friendly. No sign that anything untoward was going on.

They walked through the kitchen and into a small office. Julian gestured for Kate to take a seat.

"So, you said this was a… community thing?" Kate fished.

Julian rummaged through stacks of papers on his desk.

"Yes, we do lots of charity and community work. Edge wants to be embedded in the community, to be seen as essential as the local post office or the town hall." He paused and looked up at her sincerely. "That's the corporate spin, anyway. We *do* want to be a part of the local area, but I don't have delusions that we're as important as the post office."

Kate chuckled. "Good. I don't think many older people around here have much use for a non-fat latte, just their pension payment."

"We do have a bridge club come in every Thursday evening. When they first came, they asked me if we do ordinary tea. I said we did, and they looked so relieved. Probably convinced that we only serve plain coffee beans with a hammer and a pot of water."

"On a piece of slate," Kate added.

"Exactly!" Julian plucked out a sheet of paper. "I just

need you to fill this in. Or, as much as you can. I…
suppose you don't have an address?"

"I can use the shelter's," Kate said.

Julian handed over the piece of paper and fished
around for a pen. He didn't make eye contact, making it
obvious that this was the first time he had done anything
like this. He had the look of someone who knew they were
privileged and felt guilty about it. It was a look she had
seen a lot over the recent months.

"So, how does that work? If I may ask?" He handed
over a pen. "The shelter, I mean."

Kate started to fill in the form.

"It's a women-only shelter, only four beds. It's first
come, first served. So, I have to be there when the doors
open at nine in the evening, or I won't get a bed. They
have showers and usually a hot meal provided. Then we
have to be out at six in the morning. The space is used for
something else during the day."

"We open at seven," Julian said. "I'm usually here from
six-thirty, so you're more than welcome to come here
then."

"That would be great," Kate said. The idea of going
from the shelter to a place of work, even if unpaid, was
wonderful. "I'd need somewhere to put my sleeping bag. I
need to keep it with me… just in case."

"We have lockers, more than we need, actually, so you
can take a couple if you like," Julian offered.

Kate paused at the next question on the form. She
frowned.

"Problem?" he asked.

"This question about uniform sizes. I've not shopped

for clothes for a while. I have no idea what size I am anymore," she admitted.

"You look like you're the same size as Terri. We can have a look at her uniform and see if it fits."

Kate looked at him in surprise for a couple of moments. She hadn't realised how long it had been since she'd been treated like a normal person by a stranger. Yes, she met a lot of volunteers from various council services and charities, and most of them were lovely. But the average person she met was not.

She'd been harassed in the street by businessmen. Shouted at by drunks coming home from a night out. Sneered at by women, young and old.

Even people who tried to help were cautious, eyeing her as if she might lurch forward and bite them. It was little things, like the fact that no one wanted to touch her, or even get close to her, as if fearful she was covered in fleas, that made her feel like she was no longer a part of society.

Julian didn't seem like that. Yes, he seemed a little uncertain, but he was starting to make eye contact with her and was being polite and courteous.

"Is everything okay?" he asked.

Kate coughed and quickly focused her attention back on the form. "Yes, just… it's been a while since I've filled in paperwork."

"How long have you been… um…?"

"I've been homeless for nearly a year."

"And the council haven't done anything about it?"

"Not really, I'm on a list. In the system, as they say. But there's always someone worse off than I am. Someone who has children, or someone with medical problems, who takes priority. At least I have a roof over my head at night, most nights."

There was silence. Kate didn't blame him. If she'd been in his situation a few years ago, she wouldn't have known what to say either. It was only after living through them that she had an understanding of both sides of the coin.

"So, I suppose I should ask. Do you like coffee?" Julian asked brightly, trying to pull the conversation back on track.

"Love it," Kate admitted.

"That's good. Because once we get you on our system and go through the welcome pack, I'm going to show you how we make the best coffee in town."

———

"Well, well, well."

Kate paused wiping down a table. Her breathing quickened, and a cold chill ran down her spine. She didn't know who stood behind her, but whoever it was recognised her. It sounded like they were about to stir up all kinds of trouble.

Breathe, she reminded herself. *Just breathe.*

It was just after eight o'clock, and Edge was getting ready to close. She knew there were no other customers in the shop. Julian was in the office, and a co-worker who had introduced herself as Alena was cleaning up behind the counter.

It had been a good first day. Kate just hoped whoever stood behind her wasn't about to put a stop to that.

She stood up straight and slowly turned around.

The woman was smirking so hard Kate was afraid she'd pull a muscle. She knew that the woman recognised her, but she was having trouble identifying the woman in return. She looked somehow familiar, but months of living on the street meant she met a peculiarly high number of people.

"Do I know you?"

The woman stuck her hand out. "Selina Hale, guardian angel."

Kate politely shook her hand, quickly snatching her own hand back when the opportunity arose.

The voice shook something loose in her brain. A few seconds passed as she flicked through memories, trying to locate the woman.

Then, she remembered.

"Oh. You."

Of course, it was the rude lady from the evening before. The one with apparently forgettable nephews and a terrible attitude.

"Yes, me." She peered at the temporary name tag on Kate's apron. "Kate. I presume you want to say thank you?"

"Thank you?" Kate blinked. "For… for what?"

"Well, firstly, for the drink I kindly gave you yesterday. And, secondly." She held her hands up and gestured to the surroundings.

Kate swallowed. Her eyes flicked around the coffee shop as if taking it in for the first time. Suddenly the trendy location looked dirty, sullied.

"I spoke with Julian, recommended that he might

31

want to speak with you. Edge like to reach out and help the community. So, as your guardian angel, I thought I'd stop by and get that thank you that I didn't quite manage to hear yesterday."

Kate bit the inside of her cheek. She couldn't believe the lengths this woman—Selina—would apparently go to for a thank you. Whatever happened to doing something nice just for the sake of it?

It would have been nice to turn on her heel and leave the woman hanging, again, but Kate wasn't that foolish. Selina clearly held some sway and wasn't afraid to use it.

"I appreciate your efforts on my behalf," Kate said sweetly, determined to not actually say thank you. She wasn't going to give the woman that satisfaction.

Selina looked insanely pleased with herself. She took a breath and thrust her chest out with pride.

Kate took a small step forward, drawing herself to her full height and staring Selina right in the eye.

"I'm grateful for this opportunity and the part you played in it, but I'm not going to grovel to you. I'm not going to kiss your boots. And I'm not going to thank you every single time I see you. If you're into that kinda kink, then that's wonderful for you, but you won't get it here. This is me saying that I appreciate what you have done, Selina... what was it? Hale? I'm not going to call you my guardian angel, and I don't view you as one. Are we on the same page?"

The smirk slowly slid from Selina's face, and a cold, harsh grin replaced it. Kate didn't budge, not willing to give her a centimetre. Though Selina looked annoyed, her eyes shone with something that Kate couldn't quite place.

Grudging respect? Surely not.

"I see," Selina said. "You've made all of that very clear. I accept your gratitude and will be equally appreciative of not seeing you clogging up my car park in the future. Or, indeed, seeing you at all."

As Kate watched Selina stalk out of Edge, she wondered if she had drawn a line under the weird relationship she'd acquired with Selina. Or if this was just the beginning.

Unexpectedly Helpful

Selina marched into her office and threw her notepad onto the desk. She tossed her phone on top of it and flopped into her high-back chair. She quickly kicked her heels off and let out a long sigh.

After she'd settled into her chair, she plucked up the note from under her keyboard. She peered at it for a second, and then scrunched it up and threw it in the bin. She wasn't going to call Jeremy back any time soon.

But she was going to kill Margaret.

Who in their right mind suggested an unplanned walking tour of an event space in the middle of a meeting about office space and desk relocation?

People who want to take the heat off them and their department, she answered her own question.

Slashing marketing's budgets had happened over the last couple of weeks, and Margaret had taken it in her stride. Selina had expected an angry outburst or some kind of petty squabble, but Margaret continued to wear her annoying smile. She carried on as if the fact her department was walking wounded didn't bother her in the slightest.

But Margaret had started to cosy up to the board members. Any meeting at which a board member was present seemed to encourage the head of marketing to talk about something she knew they would enjoy hearing.

Like a client appreciation event. Because no board member would push aside a discussion about a party.

It was a brilliant strategy, right out of Selina's own playbook.

When Selina looked to cut the number of guests to an event, Margaret would talk to board members about who was on the chopping block. Obviously, her suggestions were met with panic as the board worried about upsetting their best clients who may have suddenly been uninvited.

Selina's suggestion to cut the drinks bill was met with equal concern when Margaret casually suggested they print drinks vouchers for attendees. This, the board argued, would make it appear to be a low-quality event.

And, finally, when Selina asked if they really needed to book the expensive venue everyone had their eye on, Margaret suggested they all go there to check it out. Right then. In the middle of the meeting about something else entirely.

It was only a ten-minute walk away, so of course everyone had agreed. Before long they were enjoying— some enduring—a sixty-minute tour led by the venue's event coordinator, who, Selina would avow, seemed suspiciously organised for an off-the-cuff visit.

It was seven o'clock in the evening. Gemma had, of course, gone home. Selina was behind schedule, exhausted, and starving. She'd skipped lunch with the intention of grabbing a late afternoon snack to keep her going. Now it was evening, and she knew she needed to stay to work late.

Very late.

She walked to the window and looked at the light pouring out from Edge. It was the nearest place still open and would serve food for around another hour, but she hadn't stepped foot in Edge for the last three weeks. Not since her altercation with the homeless woman, Kate.

Her stomach rumbled at the thought of a warm panini.

"Yes, yes, okay," she muttered.

She grabbed her knee-length black coat from the rack and slid her heels back on, wincing at the feel of swollen feet being crammed back into their airtight coffins. She tossed her phone into her bag and headed out.

Her dining habits were not usually dictated by strangers, but there was something about Kate that Selina couldn't quite place. Once the woman had stood up to her, Selina had felt chastised, almost embarrassed.

A sensation she was entirely unused to.

Rather than feeling smug about her solution to the car park issue, she felt empty. She'd decided to use a childish parting shot, claiming that she hoped to never see Kate again. It was something she knew she'd regret saying even as the words slipped past her lips.

Within a few minutes, she was walking through the doors and looking directly at Kate who stood behind the counter with a satisfied smirk on her face.

"Well, well, well," the woman gloated.

"Oh, you're still here?" Selina asked casually. She walked towards the display cabinet and bent to look at the food on offer.

"I am," Kate confirmed. "Didn't expect to see you here."

"Nowhere else is open," Selina said.

"That's true. But don't you have a minion to do this kind of thing for you?"

Selina stood up and made eye contact with Kate. She didn't know why she was even considering conversation with the younger woman, but it seemed pointless to ignore her. Especially considering as she'd soon be ordering food from her.

"She's pregnant and has taken to going home the very second the working day officially ends."

Kate chuckled. She turned and wiped down the work surfaces behind her. "Yep, pregnant women tend to do that," she agreed.

"She used to be rather efficient," Selina said. "Now she just waddles around like a balloon about to pop and does as little as possible."

Kate turned around, a thoughtful look on her face. "Redhead? About my height?"

"That's her. How did you know?"

"She's pregnant, and she looks like she hates her boss," Kate explained.

Selina rolled her eyes. "Yes, well, that's probably true. Can I have the brie, avocado, and tomato panini? Hot, to go."

"Sure." Kate started preparing the food. "To drink?"

Selina looked up at the menu. There were so many

options, and she was too exhausted to even think about them.

"Just… black coffee. As big a cup as possible."

"Long day?" Kate asked, plucking a large takeaway mug from the stack.

"Yes. And it will be longer still. I was stuck in a pointless meeting, which means I'll spend the next couple of hours doing the work I could have done then. Of course, I'd be getting right on with it if I had an assistant who was actually of any assistance to me." She leaned on the counter. "But instead, I'm here. With you."

"'Tis a blessing," Kate deadpanned. "Have you asked her to stay later?"

"I've indicated that someone wanting to keep their job might want to put more hours in," Selina let out a long sigh, "but it's not just the hours. Even when she is there, she's turning into a useless, fat lump."

"Endearing." The toaster started to beep. Kate skilfully removed the panini and placed it in a to-go bag. "I don't know why I'm even asking this, but have you tried to be nice? People like to help people who are nice."

"I realise you don't know me that well, but have I given you any indication that I might be nice?" Selina asked.

"I did say, 'Try to be nice,'" Kate emphasised. "Seriously, maybe you should try it. Show an interest in her pregnancy."

"But I'm *completely* uninterested."

"Yeah, I can see that. I bet she can see that, too. It's called make-believe. Show some interest. Pretend you're a human being." Kate slid the coffee and the panini across the counter and rang up the order on the till.

"You're quite rude." Selina pulled her bank card out of her purse and tapped it on the card reader.

Kate's bluntness didn't offend or faze her. In fact, she liked the honesty. But she wasn't about to sit back and accept it without a little pushback.

"I think you can handle it." Kate ripped the receipt off the till and handed it to her. "Seriously, though, consider it a test. Show some interest in her, and see how she responds. Don't go too far. We don't want her to pass out with shock or call a doctor for you."

Selina couldn't help but grin. "Very well."

She picked up her purchases and turned without another word. She was pleasantly surprised. The interaction hadn't been as terrible as she'd imagined.

Kate had obviously settled into her role well and had progressed from cleaning tables to serving customers. Selina couldn't help but feel a little pride in that. Whether she was proud of Kate for her own achievements or proud of herself for putting it all together, though, she couldn't quite tell.

7

Meeting the Family

SELINA LOOKED AT HER REFLECTION IN HER handheld mirror and attempted to tidy her hair. She hated that a simple meeting with her sister made her feel so on edge. Weren't people supposed to enjoy meeting up with their siblings?

Gemma entered Selina's office. "Margaret just dropped off the new seating plans. I pushed your meeting with Tom back to next week. He hadn't got the figures finalised, so there's no point in you wasting your time. Jonathan wants a meeting with you at Bradshaw's next Monday. You had an appointment with Sylvia, but I moved her to a later appointment on Thursday. I smoothed it over by telling her you had more time on Thursday and didn't want to hurry her along."

"Perfect." Selina slammed her compact mirror closed.

"Can I get you anything else?" Gemma asked, placing a few pieces of paper in Selina's in-tray.

"No. I'll be over at Edge with my sister if you need

me. Shouldn't take more than fifteen minutes. If I'm lucky."

After a week of dodging her sister's calls, she'd received a text saying that Abigail would meet her in a local coffee shop or else she would bring both boys into the office to meet their aunt at work.

Blackmail was Selina's go-to, so she couldn't be too angry that Abi had finally grown a backbone and used it herself.

The thought of both children running around her office—if indeed they were walking yet—was horrendous. A flurry of texts followed, and a meeting at Edge was set.

"When was the last time you saw your nephews?" Gemma asked.

Selina wasn't entirely sure. She had a vague idea of the last time she was at Abi's house, but she couldn't quite remember if the boys were there. And there was a family gathering where there were many children in attendance, but she really didn't know who was who.

But that wasn't something she was about to share with mother-to-be Gemma.

"Quite a few months ago," she said.

"Ah, it will be nice to see them and bond with them. They forget so quickly at that age."

Selina frowned. It seemed her assistant was aware of how old the children were, even if she had no idea.

"Indeed, they do," she agreed.

This new relationship with Gemma was difficult to navigate. She'd taken Kate's suggestion on board, and the very next morning had asked Gemma to sit down in her office for a few minutes under the guise of catching up.

She had asked about the pregnancy, the sex of the child—which she promptly forgot—and about preparations being made at home for the arrival. Gemma lit up and had talked without pausing for breath for more time than Selina had initially budgeted.

As Gemma spoke about clothes and nursery colours, Selina mentally prepared her day and thought about what day the following week would be best to take her car in for a service. She nodded in the right places, and then followed the most well-organised and ably assisted day in recent memory.

She wondered if it had been a fluke, and so the next day she had asked Gemma another random question about the baby, listened to another far too long response, and then enjoyed another day with an assistant who finally appeared to be awake.

Naturally, Selina was irritated that Kate had been correct, but she was happy to push that to one side and enjoy the benefits. She continued to make idle small talk with her assistant regarding her pregnancy and her useless-sounding husband.

It was hard not to fall back into old patterns, but she knew that this touch of kindness was reaping rewards, so she forged on.

"Did you finish painting the nursery last night?" Selina queried while hunting through the cupboard in her office for some shoes she didn't mind sacrificing to baby vomit. Her sister's children leaked from every orifice.

"Nearly. We think it will need another coat. That's the problem with putting a light colour over a dark colour."

"Absolutely."

Selina had no idea whether this was true or not. She hired decorators for such things. When she returned home from the office, it was either done or the decorator would return until it was done.

"I hate to mention it," Gemma said, "but Jeremy rang again. He sounded really fed up."

"He's probably exhausted from sending out invoices to me." Selina slid on some shoes. She smiled sadly at them, figuring it could be the last time she wore them.

"He told me to pass on that a court date will be inevitable unless you get back to him as soon as possible and are willing to enter negotiations with your wife."

"Ex-wife," Selina corrected.

"Ex-wife," Gemma agreed.

"Very well. Consider your message passed on."

"Will you call him?" Gemma asked.

"We'll see."

Selina grabbed her bag and coat and walked out of the office.

———

Before Selina could even step foot into Edge, Julian exited and looked at her with the pathetic lost stare of a man needing advice.

"Can I talk to you for a moment?" he asked.

Selina rolled her eyes. She didn't have time to be delayed. She had a sister to see, nephews to attempt to commit to memory, and a job to get back to.

"I don't deal with your invoices; you'll have to call Kathy in accounts." Selina tried to walk around him.

"It's not about that," he whispered.

She stopped and looked at him. He was the personification of a man stressed.

"Spit it out," she demanded.

"It's about Kate, you know, the homeless woman you told me to hire."

"I know who Kate is. It may have escaped your knowledge, but I frequent these premises three times a week. What about her?"

"Employment law states that a worker must be paid—"

"This is already sounding like something that's not my problem," Selina said. "As I believe I mentioned to you before, she needs a job. And I do rather enjoy those little bagel things that you provide when you cater one of our many, *many* meetings. Although I am aware that I have leaflets from four other businesses who would love the opportunity to quote for us. And, as much as I'd miss the bagels," she leaned in close, "I'd get over it."

Julian swallowed. "Absolutely. Understood."

He rushed to the door and opened it for her. She stepped in and looked around for Abi. She quickly saw a pram parked up in a discreet corner of the café. After a deep breath, she approached.

To her surprise, Kate was standing with her family, with a child in her arms. The child's face was red and wet. He'd clearly been engaging in some histrionics recently but now seemed to be calming down. Kate looked cool and collected, holding the boy to her in a practised grip and gently bouncing him. Her blonde hair was swept back into a ponytail, with a few strands framing her face. She looked relaxed and happy, clearly a natural with children.

"Hey, Petey, look," Kate said once she saw Selina standing there. "It's your Auntie Selina."

Petey didn't give a damn, and neither did Selina. Petey burrowed his face into Kate's shoulder and let out a wet sigh. Selina shivered at the sound.

"Hey, sis." Abi stood up and pulled her into a hug.

"Hello, blackmailer." Selina returned the hug.

"How else am I supposed to see you?" Abi turned and addressed another boy, this one playing with a racing car on the table. "Phillip, say hello to Auntie Selina."

"Hello," the boy said without looking up.

"Sorry about Peter," Abi said as she took her seat again. She gestured for Selina to take the seat opposite her. "He's been sleeping badly and throwing tantrums all over the place. Thank goodness for Kate here, she was a lifesaver."

"It was nothing," Kate said. "I love kids, and you had your hands full."

"Trying to carry a tray of drinks to the table, with a pram and these two," Abi explained.

"Sounds like a living nightmare," Selina said seriously. "Speaking of, I should get a drink. Can I get anyone anything?"

"Nonsense, I'll bring it over." Kate handed Peter back over to Abi. "You two can catch up."

Selina levelled her with a glare. "I'd like to look at the menu."

"You always order the same thing," Kate replied with a

sweet smile. "Really, I insist. Spend time with your lovely family."

Selina didn't have a chance to reply before Kate quickly left the table.

"She seems lovely. When I said I was meeting my sister here, she seemed to know it was you right away," Abi said.

"She's rather perceptive," Selina replied. She wasn't going to mention their first meeting in the car park or her snivelling little runts comment. Even if she did stand by it. She looked at Peter in Abi's arms and tried to commit his name to memory.

Peter, she reminded herself. *The smaller one is Peter.*

Not that it mattered. She knew the knowledge would vanish in no time at all. The second there was a crisis in the office, unimportant information such as this would be pushed out to make way.

It wasn't that she didn't *want* to remember. It was just hard to show interest in something she was plainly uninterested in.

Abi understood.

"So, what excuse are you going to use this time to not come to Peter's birthday?" she smiled good-naturedly.

"You know I'm very busy," Selina said.

"I do. I just wish they'd see you a little more. I want them to know you. At least be able to pick you out if you walk past them in town."

"Do they often go shopping on their own?"

"You know what I mean, Selina."

"I do." She shifted uncomfortably. Every now and then Abi pushed, and Selina still hadn't worked out how to say no to her own sister.

"How is the divorce going?" Abi suddenly asked.

"It's going."

Abi had been trying to get information out of Selina since the moment she had texted to advise her sister that Carrie was no longer a part of her life. Even though Selina made it painfully obvious that she didn't want to talk about it, or even think about it.

"Have you agreed on a settlement yet?"

"I don't see why there should be one," Selina said. "She wants to leave, she should leave. Why we should be talking about assets, my assets, is frankly beyond me. I was the one who worked all the hours, brought the money home, and managed everything. All while she was off saving the world in that ridiculously low-paying charity."

"Has she said what she wants?"

"I don't know."

"You don't know?"

"Her solicitor keeps wanting to arrange meetings. I refuse to see her, so nothing happens."

"Can't they write to you?" Abi asked.

"I assume they do. I shred correspondence from her."

Abi sighed and shook her head. "Selina, you need—"

"I'm so sorry to interrupt." Kate appeared in front of them. She glared at Selina, with something akin to fury in her eyes. It was a look Selina knew well, but she'd yet to experience it emanating from Kate. "May I speak to you? In private?"

It didn't seem like it would be a conversation Selina wanted to have, but there was a possibility that it was better than the one she was having. She stood up and gestured for Kate to lead the way.

Kate grabbed her arm and dragged her towards the window. "Did you *threaten* Julian?" she demanded.

"What?"

"Did you threaten him? To force him to give me a job?"

Selina turned around and levelled a displeased glare towards Julian, who was serving a customer at the till. When he caught Selina's glare, he sheepishly looked away.

She turned back to Kate. "I suppose it *could* be interpreted that way."

Kate's eyes bulged, and a vein in her neck started to pulsate hypnotically. Selina was fascinated by Furious Kate. The younger woman stood close, presumably in an attempt to intimidate Selina. But Selina didn't scare easily and instead appreciated the deep blue of Kate's eyes.

"He told me it was some kind of community outreach project. But it was *you*, threatening some contract. You blackmailed him!" Kate fumed.

"Then he lied to you, and your anger should be directed at him, not me. I didn't tell you that I didn't blackmail him. And I don't see the problem. You were homeless, and now you have a job. You're welcome."

"He lied because you were threatening him!" Kate whispered through clenched teeth. "He has to pay me for the work I do. It's the law."

"I fail to see the big disaster here." Selina looked back to Julian, another person to add to her hit list. How hard was it to keep his mouth shut? Now she was in the line of fire.

"He can't afford another member of staff," Kate said as if it explained everything.

Selina wasn't following along with the cryptic trail that supposedly explained Kate's rage. "The point being?"

"The point being, he is going to have to sack another member of staff in order to keep me. Because if he doesn't keep me, you'll kill a contract that the shop needs to stay afloat."

"So… you'll still be employed?"

"But someone else will lose their job," Kate said with exasperation.

"I'm really not seeing how this is an issue," Selina said.

"I'm not taking a job from someone else because you are blackmailing the manager," Kate explained. She untied her apron and tore it away from her body. "It's wrong. I won't do it."

She stalked away.

Selina shook her head and watched the proud woman until she vanished into the staff area behind the counter.

"Pride comes before the fall," she muttered.

She returned to her sister who had placed the little one —*damn, name's gone already*—into the stroller. Abi was straining her neck to see if she could see anything behind them, where Kate had disappeared.

"What was that about?" she asked, eager for gossip as usual.

"She's quitting her job," Selina said as she rejoined her sister. "Which is irritating because I got her the job in the first place. And I never got my coffee."

"Does she have another job?" Abi asked eagerly. "My au pair recently left, and we can't find a decent replacement. The agency sends people, but they are all awful. She was great with the boys the moment she saw them. Do you think she'd consider a trial period?" She stood up. "Watch the kids, I'm going to go and chat to her."

"Watch the—" Selina spluttered, but it was too late. Abi was gone.

She turned to look at the smaller one in the stroller. Somehow, he'd gone from sleepily dozing to wide awake and was now staring at her like a ticking time bomb. The bigger one continued to play with his toys.

She turned around and looked for her sister, her foolish sister who was so thrilled at the idea of help with her offspring that she was chasing after a stranger in a coffee shop. Not to mention leaving said brats with Selina while she did.

"Have I met you before?"

She turned toward the voice. The older one still wasn't looking up from where he played, but she assumed it was he who had spoken.

"Yes," she replied.

"When?" he asked.

He had her there. She had no idea.

"A while ago."

"Do you live a long way away?"

"About ten minutes by car."

He looked up at her, a small eyebrow raising in confusion.

She felt chastised. "That's a nice car," she said to try to distract from her own failings as a member of his family.

"Hmm." He turned his attention back to playing.

Abi came stalking back towards the table. "Selina," she demanded, "tell Kate that you have nothing to do with my job offer."

Selina looked at Kate, who followed in Abi's wake, looking at her suspiciously.

"This hare-brained scheme of my sister has nothing to do with me," she said truthfully.

"It isn't hare-brained," Abi said.

"You don't know this woman, and you want her to take care of your children. You met her five minutes ago," Selina pointed out.

"Well, she's already ahead of you in the queue." Abi turned to Kate. "Seriously, this has nothing do with her."

"Charming," Selina muttered.

"My au pair left to go back to Italy. The agency is sending the worst people. You're clearly good with kids, you must have experience?"

"I—I do. I used to babysit a lot in the past," Kate admitted.

"I believe you've just left your job, and I need a new nanny. This couldn't be more perfect. It's fate."

Selina rolled her eyes. Abi proclaimed everything to be fate, good or bad. To Abi, life was akin to sitting in a boat on the ocean, with waves of fate taking you wherever the tide decided. Selina preferred a boat with an engine and a compass.

"We could do a trial. You come and live with us—did I mention it's a live-in position? That won't be a problem, will it? Anyway, you could come and live with us for a week or two. And then we could talk it over and see how we all feel about it. I pay the standard industry rates. It's not much, but all your meals are included." In case Kate needed any further job perks, she added, "We have satellite TV."

Selina often wondered how her sister got through life. Hearing her negotiate with a new nanny was positively soul-destroying.

"I'm going to go and get that coffee that never showed up." She stood up and walked over to the counter. Anything to get a few precious moments away from her sister and her sister's new nanny.

She joined the lunchtime queue, for once happy to be stuck in a line. She knew that talking to Abi would either mean talking about the kids, Abi's boring husband, or her own painful divorce. Wasting as much time as possible was therefore a great option.

After a few minutes left to her own devices, she felt someone approach her.

"Did you really have nothing to do with that?"

Kate stood beside her, pinning her with a suspicious glare.

"Are you asking me if I sent my sister's au pair back to Italy and then suggested she hire a complete stranger to look after her children?"

"Well, did you?"

"No!" Selina turned away and looked at the pastry case. "I had nothing to do with it. My sister does this kind of ridiculous thing all the time. I assure you, it's her own foolish plan. I'd certainly not hire you."

"That's good, because I'd not work for you."

"Small mercies. Having one incompetent work for me is enough."

"How did that go, by the way?" Kate asked.

Selina could see her knowing grin reflected in the pastry case.

"I mean, I've noticed she's in here more and that she doesn't have that murderous look in her eye," Kate continued.

"Things are… improved," Selina allowed.

"Did you talk to her?" Kate pressed.

"I might have asked a question or two."

"So, a little kindness goes a long way?"

Selina turned to regard Kate. "You're insufferable," she said, without any feeling.

"I'm also going to be living at your sister's house for the next two weeks." Kate smirked before walking away.

The queue started to move, and Selina found herself eye to eye with Julian. He looked at her sheepishly.

"What can I get you?" he asked, a sheen of sweat across his forehead.

"A supplier with a backbone. And a black coffee."

8

A Fresh Start

KATE FOLDED THE LAST PAIR OF TINY TROUSERS AND placed them on the pile of ironed clothes. It seemed ridiculous to iron clothes for someone as young as Peter, but it was something Abigail wanted and so Kate was happy to do it.

It was her third day in the expensive house in the posh end of Parbrook, and she already felt like one of the family. She couldn't believe how quickly she had managed to settle in nor how nice Abigail and Michael were.

Michael worked long hours, so she rarely saw him. Abigail worked part time at an office and also spent time volunteering for the local church. Kate was still getting to know her, but on first glance she seemed like a typical middle-class mum. She was ruled by what the other mums said was in or out of fashion and spent a ridiculous amount of time setting up pictures for social media. A casual shot of the average day at home took around an hour to prepare.

Appearance was important for Abigail. She wanted to

come across as the perfect mum with well-turned-out kids, a nanny, a nice home, a job, and a role with the church. Which was why Kate was fairly sure that Abigail had no idea that Kate used to be homeless. Or that Kate *would be* homeless if she wasn't living in the guest bedroom of the house.

Kate didn't feel comfortable keeping the information from Abigail. She deserved to know who was looking after her kids, but there hadn't been a good time to discuss it. And Abigail spoke a hundred miles an hour, often changing the subject three times in one sentence.

Kate had managed to put away some money from her job at Edge, once she had passed a certain number of days and Julian was legally obligated to pay her a small salary. It was more money than she'd had in months, but it still wasn't enough to do anything practical. She needed much more to put a deposit down on her own place and to start to pay her own way again. She'd had plenty of time to calculate what she needed to pay a deposit as well as rent and bills, and buy the bare essentials. A year ago, that figure would have been large but manageable. Now it seemed impossible.

The money Abigail would pay her would help her reach that goal, though. It would help her finally be financially independent again.

It had always seemed like a dream, something completely removed from reality, but she was slowly moving toward her goal. Her salary as a live-in nanny wasn't much. Having a roof over her head and all her food and bills paid for was great, but the small salary meant it would take many, many months to save anything usable.

So, Kate meant to stay with Abi and her family for as long as she could. The safety of a job and a roof over her head were a blessing. She just hoped that when she finally did tell Abi about her former status, she wouldn't be back on the streets in a flash.

She kept telling herself that she wasn't really keeping her homelessness a secret in order to bide her time and save money, but she knew that if she'd really wanted to tell Abigail, she would have been able to by now.

"Nicole has a new car," Abigail announced, walking into the utility room with her phone in her hand. "She kept that one quiet. She must have ordered it weeks ago; it has a custom paint job. That's so cheeky. I bet she wanted to get one over on Jackie because she recently had the outside of the house repainted. Wait, I have a picture. You tell me what you think of this."

Abigail swiped and stabbed at the screen. She turned the phone and held it out for Kate to see. The house looked fine to Kate, but Abigail pulled a face of disgust.

"Ostentatious," Kate said, guessing that was Abigail's issue.

"Precisely!" She turned her phone around and shook her head. "Completely out of keeping with the area. Trying to draw attention to the double extension, which she didn't get planning permission for. She's lucky that Julie didn't say anything. Well, she wouldn't because we'd all know it was Julie."

"Julie's like that?" Kate asked while putting more laundry on.

"Oh, yes! She reports everything everyone does. I bet the council and the police have their own file for her. She can't keep her nose out of people's business. Here's the picture of Nicole's new car." She spun the phone around again to show a shiny sports car on a driveway.

Kate looked and nodded. "Nice car."

"It is. Michael says we can't get one because of the kids. Apparently, it's not practical, but I go out plenty of times without the kids. It would be nice to do it in a car that I like." Abigail turned the phone off and tossed it onto the pile of ironing. "Selina had the same model before the car she has now. I asked her to let me know if she was selling it, but she didn't. Typical. Probably wouldn't have given me a deal on it anyway."

"Doesn't sound like something she'd do."

"No. She's nice enough. To me. When I make her. But she's, well, she's Selina."

Kate knew exactly what Abigail meant, even from the few short meetings she'd had with the woman. She was simply... Selina.

"Do you see her often?"

Abigail laughed. "No. I have to force her to come over or meet me somewhere. It's great since the boys have been around. I can threaten to bring them to her office. She'll do anything to avoid that. She's not great with kids. Any kids. Not just mine. You'd think she'd make an effort with her own flesh and blood, but no."

"Has she always been like this?" Kate asked.

"Yes. The moment she was old enough to leave home she did. She got a part-time job and paid her way through higher education. Started working as soon as she could and basically committed her life to her job."

Kate opened her mouth to reply but paused. She could

hear the sound of Peter waking up from his afternoon nap. She pressed the button on the washing machine and started to make her way to the stairs.

"That's my cue," she said as she passed Abigail.

"You're an angel. I have so much to be getting on with!"

As Kate climbed the stairs, she heard Abigail on the phone, asking someone if they'd seen the picture of the new car. She smiled and shook her head. This new job was certainly an interesting one.

It was nice to be considered part of a family again, even if she was paid to be there. She wondered if she'd just stay until she had enough money to move on, or if she'd stay on until the boys were too old to need her.

She smiled at the thought of being somewhere for so long.

It was nice to have options again.

9

The Unfamiliar Aunt

KATE WAS SITTING ON THE FLOOR OF THE NURSERY, playing with the boys. The expansive five-bedroom house was pure luxury, and Kate wondered if the kids would ever realise how lucky they were to have a bedroom each and a shared playroom in between. Probably not, as they'd no doubt end up socialising with children from similar backgrounds.

Abigail came into the room with a confused look on her face and her phone held loosely in her hand.

"Everything okay?" Kate asked.

"My sister is coming over," she replied, looking like she didn't quite believe it herself.

"Oh." Kate didn't know what to make of the news. She'd gathered that Selina never visited unless she was practically forced to. She wondered if it had something to do with her. Maybe Selina had decided that her sister needed to know the truth about Kate.

Her palms felt clammy. She rubbed them on her jeans.

She knew she should have been honest with Abigail

sooner, admitted that she'd been homeless when she first met Selina, but all her good intentions had vanished as she became more settled into the Brownlow family.

It had been three weeks. Both Kate and Abigail had agreed that everything was working out beautifully, and Kate had agreed to stay on permanently as the boys' au pair. The weekly pay meant that Kate actually had money. Not a lot, but enough to buy some new clothes and other personal bits and pieces. Which she desperately needed because Abigail was starting to notice that Kate only had three outfits.

Kate got to her feet. "Did she say why she was coming over?"

"Aunt Selina's coming over?" Phillip asked.

"She is." Abigail tried to look enthusiastic but couldn't quite manage to lose her confused expression. "Something about paperwork. She said she'd be here within the hour."

Maybe nothing to do with me then, Kate mused. She looked down at the boys. "I think we should get changed into some nicer clothes. Won't that be fun?"

Phillip shrugged. Peter ignored her and continued to play with his toys.

"Good idea," Abigail said. "I'll go and get changed, too. And see if I have that tea she likes."

She vanished in a cloud of near-panic.

"Why do I have to get changed?" Phillip asked.

"Because you got a little grubby when we went to the park this morning, and we don't want your aunt to think you're grubby." Kate opened the chest of drawers and started digging for the smart shirt and vest combination his mother dressed him in for photos the previous week. Both the children had so many clothes that there was an overspill into the nursery. Considering their clothes were tiny, Kate guessed the boys had more clothes than she had ever had throughout the course of her life.

"Why?" Peter asked.

"Why" was his favourite word. His current state of mind was to question everything. Repeatedly.

Luckily, Kate was patient and enjoyed talking to him and answering all of his bizarre questions.

"Because we want to look our best. So, people think, 'Wow, they were really nice-looking.'" Kate handed the clothing to Phillip.

He pulled a face. "But I don't like Aunt Selina."

Kate crouched down and looked him in the eye. "You don't *know* Aunt Selina. Not liking someone is different to not knowing much about them."

Phillip scrunched up his face while he considered her point. After a few seconds, he nodded and turned away to get changed.

It hurt Kate to think that Selina and her nephews may never have a connection. That neither would really get the chance to know the other.

Of course, the blame lay squarely at Selina's door.

Peter picked up a plastic building block and lifted it into the air. He bit the inside of his cheek as he stared hard at his brother's back. Kate chuckled. Luckily Peter was at the age where hand-eye coordination needed a little while to engage after the brain sent the signal of a potential good idea.

She snatched the block out of his hand before he

launched it into his brother. Peter looked at her and giggled.

"Caught you," she admonished him. "None of that. We have to get you changed as well."

Peter blew a long, loud raspberry.

"That's what I say when I have to do something I don't want to do, too," Kate agreed.

———

The family gathered in the living room to await Selina's arrival. Abigail sat on the edge of the sofa while Peter and Phillip played with a jigsaw puzzle which comprised of large, foam pieces. Kate decided the jigsaw was the safest bet. Both boys could play together, it was unlikely to cause an argument, and it was blissfully silent.

"I don't know what I'm worried about," Abigail announced as she fretted with her hands. "I'm sure it's nothing. Just so unusual. Unless…"

"Unless?" Kate pushed, concern eating at her. Would Selina really be cruel enough to wait for Kate to relax in her new role before sweeping in and spilling all her secrets?

"Unless it's something about the divorce." Abigail whispered the word "divorce" as if her two- and four-year-old would be scarred for life by a term they surely wouldn't understand.

The doorbell rang, and Abigail jumped to her feet.

"Remember to say hello to your aunt," Kate told the boys. Typically, the children would ignore the arrival of people they didn't know or like, but she wanted to try to form some kind of connection between them and Selina if she could.

Two heads nodded without looking up.

She heard some mumbled greetings in the hallway, and couldn't help shake the dizzy feeling that she was about to have everything snatched away from her. Selina could be mean, she knew that based upon their very first encounter, but she didn't know if Selina was vindictive enough to go out of her way to ruin her life.

Selina entered the living room, almost looking surprised to see Kate.

"You remember Kate." Abigail walked in behind her sister. "Boys, look who's here."

The boys both looked up and mumbled half-hearted hellos.

Kate offered an awkward wave, not really knowing what else to do. Selina looked uncomfortable as she nodded a formal greeting to the boys, who had already returned to playing.

Noting that her arrival hadn't interested the boys in the slightest, she set her gaze on Kate. "You're settling in well?"

It seemed like a genuine enquiry, and so Kate nodded. "I am."

"Good." Selina turned awkwardly towards her sister. "Can we talk?"

"Sure, come through to the kitchen. I have that tea you like." Abigail gestured towards the next room, and they both left.

Kate felt confused. She had no idea why Selina was visiting out of the blue, but it didn't seem to have anything to do with her. Otherwise, she wouldn't have asked if she were settling in.

Or would she?

Not knowing was driving Kate insane. She didn't want to eavesdrop, but she needed to know if Selina was about to place a ticking time bomb in the middle of her happy new life.

The boys were contentedly getting on with their puzzle, so Kate took the opportunity to move to the chair closest to the kitchen. The sound of the kettle muted the sisters' murmuring conversation.

Kate's heart started to pound in her chest until that was all she could hear. She hated that she was listening in on a private conversation. She hated that she hadn't be honest with Abigail from the start. She'd known she should have mentioned her background and explained everything, but the possibility that Abigail wouldn't under-stand and wouldn't want to take a risk on her was too great.

The kettle started to near the end of its cycle and built to a crescendo before going quiet.

"She's a monster," she heard Selina say.

Kate felt instantly cold. It was like someone had thrown a bucket of ice water over her. Her hands gripped the arms of the chair.

"You're over-exaggerating," Abigail replied neutrally.

"If you knew what I knew—"

"I'd still say you were exaggerating," Abigail cut her off. "Carrie hurt you, and now you don't have any perspective on the matter."

Carrie? Kate frowned. *Who on earth is Carrie?*

"I have plenty of perspective," Selina argued.

"If you say so," Abigail said doubtfully. "Not that I'm not pleased to see you, but may I ask why you are here?"

"I need to talk to you about the divorce."

It seemed that Abigail had been right; the unexpected visit was something to do with a divorce. Kate couldn't imagine being married to someone like Selina. Sure, she was attractive, held down a good job, and looked like she had money, but *living* with her? She shivered at the thought.

Her mind drifted back to her own failed marriage, and took back her shiver when she realised Selina would have been a walk in the park in comparison.

"I thought you didn't want to talk about the divorce," Abigail said.

"That was then, now I do," Selina replied. "Now that Carrie is forcing my hand."

"I'm not surprised. The longer you ignored her—"

"I know, I know. I just need your help to sign some paperwork to prevent her from getting her hands on my assets. And I've realised that going to court won't benefit me. I thought I'd get a fair trial, but some research has indicated that I won't."

"So now you don't want to go to court?" Abigail confirmed.

"No. The legal system is flawed."

"Have you even spoken to her since she moved out?" Abigail asked.

"No. Why would I?"

"Because she's your wife."

"Ex-wife."

"Not yet."

The rest of the conversation faded out as Kate repeated the word "ex-wife" over and over in her head. Selina was interested in women.

Kate felt her heart lift.

Kate's own sexuality had been the reason her life had been torn to shreds. Knowing that someone like Selina was successful and out of the closet was life-affirming for her.

Logically, she knew there were plenty of people who were open about their sexuality and living happy, prosperous lives, but she'd yet to meet one. By the time Kate had come to realise she preferred women, it was far too late for her. Memories of the past shouldered past the walls she had built in her mind, walls she'd constructed to stop herself reliving the painful events that led to a life on the streets.

"Kate?"

She blinked and looked up to see Abigail looking down at her. It looked like she had been saying her name a few times.

"Sorry, I was miles away," Kate apologised.

Abigail laughed. "No problem, I was just asking if you wanted a cuppa?"

"No, I'm fine, thank you."

Peter stumbled over to Kate and fell into her lap. "Read to me?"

Kate laughed. "See? No time for tea, I have to read to this young gentleman."

Abigail mussed Peter's hair and smiled fondly at him. "Okay, give me a call if you need anything."

Kate picked him up and stood. She wondered if the toddler had any idea how lucky he was to be in such an accepting family. Abigail clearly loved her sister, even if Selina seemed to be hard work most of the time. She pushed aside her own feelings of inadequacy and abandonment and held the boy a little tighter.

"Let's go and find a book, shall we?" she asked him. "Coming, Phillip?"

Phillip abandoned the jigsaw quickly and raced after them as she carried Peter towards the nursery.

———

It was an hour later when Kate heard someone climbing the stairs. She'd been playing with the kids and engaging Phillip in his usual bonkers conversations, but her mind had been distracted.

Selina was gay. And lived a good life. Okay, so she was a bitch and had no idea how to treat people and certainly could not be considered a role model. But she was gay, out, and she wasn't treated any differently as far as Kate could tell.

She noticed someone in the doorway to the nursery and assumed it was Abigail.

"I'll put Peter down for his nap in a while," Kate said.

"That's the small one?"

She snapped her head around. Selina was in the doorway, looking at the boys with a frown. She looked a little tired, like sleep hadn't come easily recently, but she still looked gorgeous in her skirt suit, heels, and swept-back hair. She looked competent and ready to deal with anything. Kate wondered if the tiredness was simply something she allowed herself to show now that she was out of the office.

Was this Selina with her guard slightly down? Did Selina ever really let her guard down?

"Yes. Peter and Phillip, as you well know." Kate pointed to each boy individually as she said their names. She wanted Selina to know who was who but not let the boys know that their aunt had no idea. "Your aunt Selina does like to joke around, doesn't she, boys? She'll be calling me Kimberly soon."

Phillip smiled, instantly accepting that it was all a joke. Peter carried on sleepily stacking building blocks.

"Of course, I'm known for my jokes." Selina stepped a hesitant foot into the room. "Abi is on the phone to her putrid..." She paused and looked at the boys for the moment as if realising that she was about to put her foot in it. "I thought I'd leave her in private while she takes the call."

"You're always welcome here," Kate said.

Selina stepped forward again. It was as if she were edging closer to wildcats in a zoo enclosure. "So, boys, how is school?" she asked.

"Phillip starts school next year," Kate explained. She didn't mention that Peter was three years away from being school age, though she suspected that Selina had no idea of that fact.

There was no doubt in her mind that Selina could deal with any work-related issue. She was intelligent and driven. But when it came to children, family, and even personal matters, Selina seemed clueless.

In some ways, it was adorable. Seeing the powerful businesswoman struggle to put an age on a child was entertaining.

"Oh. Well. How do they fill their days?"

Phillip stood up and rushed past Selina, on the way to his bedroom. Peter noticed he was alone with the strange new woman and quickly followed him out of the room.

Selina let out a sigh. She looked at Kate. "They hate me."

"Well, they don't *know* you." Kate started to tidy the nursery. "And you make no effort to know them, I suspect."

"No, I don't," she admitted. "I don't know how to talk to children."

"You're not great with adults either," Kate pointed out.

"This is true." Selina picked up a book from the floor and looked it over.

"Do you really want some kind of a relationship with them? Or is this to fill two minutes while your sister is on the phone?" Kate asked.

Selina looked at the back of the book, seemingly contemplating the question. After a few moments she looked up. "I'd like some kind of connection. I don't want them staying at my house and getting their grubby hands everywhere." She shuddered. "But something... yes. It would make Abi happy."

"Then do what you did with your assistant, show some interest."

"I don't feel like we have the same conversational points. I doubt either of them have tried the new Italian in town." Selina put the book on a shelf. "What does one say

69

to children? 'Nice weather we're having? Going on any holidays this year?'"

Kate put her hands on her hips and stared at Selina.

"What?" Selina asked.

"Look around you." Kate gestured around the room.

Selina followed her hand. "It's a nursery."

"They spend all of their time in here. *This* is their interests in one room." Kate pointed to the bookshelf. "They like reading. And jigsaw puzzles. Peter likes cuddly teddy bears, and Phillip likes toy cars. Everything you need to know about them is right here. They aren't secretive or difficult to figure out, you just need to look."

Selina frowned and looked at the shelves. She started to walk around the room, slowly examining everything her eyes came across, as if seeing things for the first time.

Kate watched her. She couldn't quite understand Selina. She couldn't tell her nephews apart, but there seemed to be a sadness within her as well. As if she wanted to connect but didn't know how. It made her realise how little she understood the woman in front of her.

"Will you tell Abigail about me?" Kate blurted out.

Selina didn't even pause her examination of the shelves. "Tell her what?"

"About me… being homeless," Kate whispered.

Selina stopped and turned to face her. "I hadn't intended to. Do you want me to?"

"I… I'd rather you didn't."

Selina shrugged and turned back to exploring the toys. "Then I won't."

"Thank you. It's just… I'm not keeping it a secret. Well, I am. But only because—"

"Because you fear the judgement," Selina surmised. "I understand. I have no intention of telling Abi. She hired you based on a three-minute conversation in a coffee shop. It's not up to me to do due diligence for her."

The dig at her sister was obvious, but Kate couldn't help but be relieved that Selina seemed willing to keep her secret. She knew she'd have to tell Abigail soon, but at least this way she could pick the right moment.

"However, I do have a question." Selina turned to look at Kate again.

"Sure?"

"Julian told me that you had been homeless for almost a year?"

Kate nodded, although she was surprised that Selina had talked to Julian about her. She wondered why, curious as to how that topic of conversation had come up. And, more importantly, who had brought it up.

"And yet, you only recently started spending your days in the car park behind my office."

"Oh, yes, I moved there. It was safer, you know?"

Selina shook her head. Inquisitive eyes bored into her. "No, I don't know."

Kate took a deep breath. This wasn't something she wanted to be talking about, especially not with Abigail or the kids potentially lurking around any corner.

"I'd been in a few different places," Kate admitted. "Sometimes there's safety in numbers, so people hang out in the same area. Sometimes, that's not such a good idea, and it's better to be alone."

Selina's expression didn't change. She looked genuinely interested, but not pitying. She looked like she was going to ask a follow-up question but stopped herself. She tilted her head towards the door, hearing something.

"Abi's off the phone. We'll park this conversation for now, but rest assured that I won't be saying anything of your previous circumstances." Selina walked towards the door, then paused. "And thank you, for the advice regarding the children."

Kate didn't get a chance to say anything. Selina glided into the hallway and back downstairs to her conversation with her sister.

10

Seeking Advice

GEMMA ENTERED SELINA'S OFFICE AND PLACED THE morning post on her desk.

"Good morning, how are you today?" she asked.

Selina looked up from her laptop screen. The truth was that she was tired and stressed, but that was most days lately. In fact, for as long as she could really remember, that had been the case. Having the weight of the company's internal operations on her shoulders was exhausting. Not that she could complain as she had spent years wrestling responsibility from other people in order to ensure tasks were done properly.

She swept her own feelings to one side. She had goals to meet, and that was the most important thing. Rest would come. Once she was on the thirteenth floor, she'd assist in recruiting her replacement. That poor soul would then get her workload dumped on them, and Selina would spend her days in board meetings or having networking lunches with the City bigwigs.

It would all be worth it in the end.

"Good," she finally answered. "And you?"

Gemma grimaced a little. Selina knew without asking that the young woman was still struggling to sleep through the night, owing to her athletic unborn child's regular dance recitals.

She didn't know how Gemma managed pregnancy. Selina was certain that she would only be able to survive on so little sleep with an enormous amount of coffee to get her through the day, and that option wasn't open to expectant mothers like Gemma. Nor was demolishing a decent bottle of red before bed to ensure a good night's sleep.

And, after all of that hassle, she and her husband would be saddled with a screaming baby for years. Then a grumpy teenager. Then a miserable adult. Forever.

"My sister used to sprinkle lavender mist on her pillow," Selina suggested. She only knew Abi did so because they'd met for lunch one day and she realised her sister smelt like their grandmother had done.

"Oh, I heard something about that," Gemma said. "I'll give it a try, thanks! Can I get you anything?"

Selina shook her head. "No, I'm doing a deep dive into these figures. So, no interruptions, if possible."

"Absolutely." Gemma turned and left the office, closing the door on her way out.

Selina turned her attention back to her laptop. Just as she started to focus again, her mobile beeped with a text message.

She'd meant to turn it to silent but had forgotten. She sighed, knowing she'd never be able to focus now that she knew there was an unread text.

She grabbed her phone and glanced at the note. A

smile tugged at the corners of her mouth. She read the message twice, enjoying its contents.

Hey sis, just wanted to say thank you for sending the box of presents for the boys. They really loved it! You're the talk of the town in our house this morning x Come over sometime, they'd love to see you. Abi x

A breath she didn't even know she was holding escaped her lips. She'd thought for a while about whether or not to reach out to the children in some way. She wanted to be something to them. What, she wasn't entirely sure. She didn't fit into family life in a neat and tidy way.

A picture of Kate gesturing to items in the boy's nursery had entered her mind. She knew that she'd never have put the pieces together without Kate's guidance.

Her eyes drifted up and looked at Gemma on the other side of the glass wall. Kate had helped her there, too. Showing a little kindness to Gemma had changed her working environment beyond recognition. And the more she showed an interest in Gemma and her impending doom—er, motherhood—the more helpful Gemma became.

A sharp knock on the door followed by a gust of wind as it flew open shocked her from her thoughts.

Jeremy Lovejoy stood in the doorway. His trench coat was slung over his arm, his briefcase gripped tightly in his hand. He was practically scowling.

"Not now, I'm extremely busy." Selina lowered her phone and returned her attention to her laptop.

"Selina, we have to talk about the divorce," Jeremy said. He invited himself into the office, closing the door and taking a seat in front of her.

"I'm sure I hired you to deal with it." She refused to look up.

"And I'd love to. But you don't answer calls. Or emails. Or letters. I'd try a carrier pigeon, but I'm not sure that would have much luck either."

She slammed her laptop closed. "Remind me, are your bills up to date?"

"Yes."

"Fully paid? On time?"

"Yes." He rolled his eyes.

"So, I'm paying you. I don't see what the issue is." She leaned back and pinned him with her harshest glare.

"The problem is that you won't let me do the job you are paying me to do. You want this divorce, correct?"

"Of course I do," she scoffed.

"Then we have to work together. You have to communicate with me. And, I'm sad to say, you have to communicate with your wife."

"Ex-wife."

"Wife," Jeremy ground out. "She is your wife and will remain your wife until you start the negotiation process."

Selina lifted the laptop lid. "I'm too busy to discuss this now."

Jeremy leaned forward and pushed the laptop closed. "Things need to be discussed. I can't do what you're asking me. I can't just grant you a divorce without your input. As painful as this is, things need to be agreed upon. Conversations must be had."

Selina glared at the offending hand that had slammed the lid of the computer, narrowly missing her fingers. "Jeremy, I—"

He stood up. "I'm giving you one week. If you haven't replied to my email from this morning by then, I'm going to have to drop you as a client and advise you find other representation."

"But—"

"One week." He left the office before she could say another word.

She stared at the doorway in shock. Jeremy Lovejoy had been her solicitor for years. His firm had worked with her father long before. He was a man she could rely on, and now he was issuing threats.

Gemma appeared in the doorway looking contrite. "I'm sorry, he just stormed in."

"It's fine." She opened her laptop again and stared at the screen, determined to look unaffected by Jeremy's behaviour. She didn't know if she fooled Gemma or not, but it was all she could do. Her thoughts whirred, and she couldn't focus. One thing she knew for certain: she was not about to have a meltdown in her office. That couldn't happen.

Glass-partitioned offices had their uses. However, Selina often felt like she was on display in a cabinet for all to see. Ordinarily that wasn't a problem, but right now she felt as though the whole office was sneaking glances at her.

She slammed the laptop closed.

"On second thought, Gemma, I'm going to work from

home today. There are just too many distractions here, and I need to fully focus on this. Forward all calls to my mobile. And move my meetings." Selina was already on her feet and packing her belongings into her bag.

Gemma wisely did as she was asked without comment.

Selina was fuming. Angry at Jeremy. Angry at her ex. Angry at the world. And she didn't know what to do about it.

11

Some Advice

THE DOORBELL RANG, AND KATE LET OUT A SIGH. IT was her day off. Abigail was out with the boys, allowing Kate some much needed quiet time. She loved the kids, but they were very noisy. Even after they had left the house, she felt as if her ears continued to ring for a while.

Once Abigail had left, Kate had enjoyed a long, hot shower. Afterwards, she'd put on some comfortable clothes and made herself some coffee from the luxurious machine in the kitchen.

She'd only taken one sip when the doorbell sounded. She briefly considered leaving it, considering her wet hair and torn joggers and T-shirt. But it might have been important, so she walked into the hallway and peeked through the peephole in the front door.

Selina stood on the other side. She wore a smart trouser suit, looking like she'd come straight from her office. She also looked anxious, shifting from one foot to another.

Kate opened the door. "Um, hi. Abigail is out with the boys."

Selina rolled her eyes and started to turn around to leave.

"Can I help?" The question left her lips before she'd properly considered it. Of course she couldn't help. Selina had obviously come to visit her sister, not her, but seeing her so on edge made Kate want to reach out.

Selina stopped, still facing away from her. Kate noticed her slumped shoulders.

"I've finally figured out the coffee machine. It's nearly as good as the one at Edge," she offered.

Selina turned around and regarded her for a few moments.

Kate suddenly felt small, standing in the doorway of a grand house where she was essentially nothing more than the help. Wearing old, torn clothes, her wet hair hanging messily on her shoulders.

Selina was her opposite in every single way. Meticulously put together, sporting a designer suit, not a hair out of place, immaculate makeup.

"I'd like that," she finally said, surprising Kate.

"Oh, right, great." Kate stood to one side and gestured for Selina to enter the house.

"What can I get you? Black coffee? Latte?" Kate asked once they were both in the kitchen.

"A latte sounds appealing," Selina said. She placed her bag on the floor and sat on one of the stools at the kitchen island.

"Coming right up." Kate quickly set about making the drink, adding a little kick because she knew Selina was a coffee snob and enjoyed a strong beverage. "Sorry you missed Abigail."

"It's fine. I'm not really sure why I'm here. I doubt she could have been much use."

"Is there anything I can help with?" Kate asked again hesitantly.

Selina gave a light laugh. "Only if you can grant me an immediate divorce from my ex-wife without my having to speak with her. Apparently, it's completely impossible for the legal system to do its job. I either have to sit down and mediate with her, or I have to go to court. And, apparently, I wouldn't do well in court."

Kate marvelled at how easy it was for Selina to step out of the closet. She spoke about her wife, ex-wife, as if it were nothing out of the ordinary. Kate wished that she had lived a life where that was true for her. She would give anything to be so casually out and not have to worry about what that meant, what people might think about it.

She turned. "Why don't you want to speak to her?"

Selina blinked. "Because she… she left. She just walked out. Completely out of the blue. And now I'm expected to split my assets with her. Pay her… danger money for having to live with me."

"What does she want, if I may ask?"

"I don't know," Selina said flippantly. "Everything, probably."

"But you don't know?"

"Not a clue. As I say, I don't want to speak with her."

Kate leaned back against the work surface. "So, there's a possibility that she doesn't want anything?"

"Unlikely," Selina scoffed.

"But you don't know. You have no idea what she wants or doesn't want?"

Selina sat up straight and looked at the clock on the wall. "When will my sister be back?"

Kate shook her head and chuckled. "She'll tell you the same thing."

"I'm the injured party here," Selina argued. "Why should I do something I categorically don't want to do? Why should I have to sit in a room with her?"

"Because life is unfair, and sometimes we have to do stuff we don't want to do." Kate turned and finished up making the latte. She placed it in front of Selina. "How long have your divorce proceedings been going on?"

Selina pulled the cup and saucer towards her. Her face scrunched into a contemplative look. "A year?" she guessed.

Kate blinked. "A year?"

"Give or take."

"A year, twelve months?" Kate clarified.

"Things move slowly in the legal world. It can be a month between letters," Selina defended.

"And you've not spoken to her in all that time?"

"No."

"Don't you just... want it to be over?" Kate asked. She couldn't imagine having that hanging over her for so long. Constantly having to deal with solicitors. Still being married, unable to move on with her life.

"Well, yes," Selina agreed. "But at what cost?"

"May I ask how long you were married?"

"Three years."

That surprised Kate. Selina was older, Kate wasn't

quite sure of her exact age. It was difficult to pinpoint as Selina took very good care of herself. For some reason Kate had assumed this had been a marriage of many years. Kate was considerably younger than Selina, and her own marriage had lasted much longer.

She shuddered at the memory.

"Three years? She can't expect to get that much out of a settlement for such a short marriage," Kate mused. "You've probably spent more in solicitor fees over the last year than what she is asking for. Which might be nothing."

Selina sipped the latte. "I suppose you think I should talk to her? Presumably I should fake interest in her, as you suggested I do with Gemma."

"Well, that worked. And the boys loved the presents you sent. They keep asking when you'll be coming to visit next," Kate replied.

Selina's eyes brightened a little at that.

Kate smiled. It was nice to see a bridge forming between aunt and nephews. Selina had to be the one to make the effort, and she'd done so brilliantly, much to Kate's surprise. It had paid off, and Selina was rightly pleased with herself.

"Which you should do, by the way," Kate continued the thought. "You can buy children's love, but it's a limited time offer and requires a little upkeep."

"I'll arrange something with Abi," Selina said through a hard-done-by sigh which Kate didn't quite believe. She sipped her latte again, looking at Kate over the rim of the cup. "Do you?"

"Do I what?" Kate asked, confused by the topic change.

"Do you think I should talk to her?"

Kate hadn't expected Selina to ask her for advice. It felt like something reserved for family input only. But this wasn't the first time that Selina had sought Kate's advice, nor the first time she had followed it with successful results.

Now the pressure was on. Of course, she thought Selina should speak with her ex, but Selina was obviously very against the idea.

"I think, if you want this to be over sooner and to move on with your life, it would be less heartache for you to get it over and done with," she said diplomatically. "I know you don't want to talk to her, but in the interest of getting it done and moving on… you might have to."

Selina silently nodded before taking another sip of her drink. It reminded Kate that she had been drinking her own coffee. She snatched up the mug from the counter and took a few big gulps.

A couple of minutes went by before Selina spoke again. "You're enjoying your role here?"

Kate was again taken aback by the change in topic but quickly caught up. It seemed to be a trait of Selina's to flip from topic to topic as it suited her. Kate wondered if that was a habit of someone who rarely engaged in casual conversation.

"Yes, I love it. The boys are great, so is Abigail." She licked her suddenly dry lips. "I've still not found the opportunity to tell her about… you know."

"Your previous situation?" Selina guessed.

"Exactly. I mean, I will. I just… It was never the right time. And now I feel like too much time has passed. I don't wish to be dishonest. But—"

Selina waved her hand casually. "You don't need to explain yourself to me. I'm sure if you had planned to rob my sister, then you would have done so by now. Besides, as I said before, it's nothing to do with me."

Kate wanted to argue, wanted to point out that it did have something to do with Selina as Abigail was her family, but she decided that it was in her best interests not to stress the point too much. She still felt guilty for not telling Abigail the truth. The fact was, there hadn't been much time. Abigail was always busy, or the boys needed her attention.

Not to mention the little voice at the back of Kate's head that constantly reminded her that one false move could have her kicked out.

"Are Abi and Michael treating you well?" Selina asked.

Kate nodded quickly. "Abi is lovely. So is Michael, I just don't see him very often. He is always away with business."

Selina snorted a laugh. "Yes, he is very busy with *business*."

Kate didn't know what Selina meant by that. Didn't want to know.

"So, you're happy here?" Selina continued.

"I am. It wasn't where I saw myself, but then nothing has been what I imagined for the last few years." Kate held the mug of lukewarm coffee tightly.

Selina eyed her grip. "I can't imagine," she admitted. "I don't think I'd last very long on the streets. Certainly not for a whole year. Although I can't imagine why you were homeless for so long. I pay taxes, I see council homes going to vulnerable families. Why were you left on the streets to fend for yourself for such a long time?"

Kate's heart felt warm with the anger in Selina's tone. Her soft rage was pointed at those who hadn't supported Kate in her time of need. It felt good to know someone was on her side.

"I wasn't prioritised," Kate explained. "I had access to a shelter. I didn't have any children. I wasn't on drugs, no health issues. All those people go to the top of the list."

"For a whole year?" Selina was incredulous.

"There's a lot of homeless people. Not enough emergency housing to go around." Kate drank the last of her coffee. "And every time they cleared the most at risk and put them in housing, more arrived on that list. I never really progressed up the ladder. But I had the shelter most of the time."

"Tell me about this shelter." It was an instruction more than a request. Some might have considered it rude, but Kate knew it was just Selina's way. Professional, no nonsense.

"It's a woman-only shelter," Kate recited. She'd had to explain her situation more than once and practically had a script these days. "Four beds. Opens at nine in the evening, closes at six in the morning. First come, first served. I managed to get in there most nights. They have some hot food, a decent bed, and access to showers."

"Did you ever not get in?" Selina asked, getting straight to the point.

"A couple of times," Kate confessed. "Didn't get there

in time, or the shelter couldn't open because there weren't enough volunteers."

"And then?" Selina pressed at the on-going silence.

"Then I'd sleep by the bus station, or by the bridge on the abandoned railway line. It depended who was around." Kate quickly turned away from Selina and washed her mug. She didn't want to think about those times.

"Most of the time, though, I was at the shelter. It was a good place," she said brightly, trying to convince both herself and Selina that it was all okay.

"I see."

It was quiet for a few moments. Only the sound of the kitchen tap running filled the growing hush.

"I should be going," Selina finally said. "Tell Abi I'll call her later and will advise a time to come over and see the boys. When is Michael home?"

"Thursday."

"Good, I need to speak to him about Abi's upcoming birthday."

Kate looked at Selina. "She didn't mention her birthday. When is it?"

"The eighteenth. She doesn't like a lot of fuss. Michael and I usually arrange a quiet family meal or something. I presume this year will be no different. If he can be bothered to turn up."

Kate didn't say anything. She knew that Michael's constant absence with work was something Abigail struggled with. Kate just attempted to stay as neutral as possible.

"Enjoy your…" Selina looked Kate up and down,

reminding her what a state she probably looked. "Day off?"

"Yes. I don't normally dress like this," Kate said.

"I should think not." Selina grabbed her bag and showed herself out of the kitchen. "It would scare the children."

Kate chuckled. "Always a pleasure, Selina," she called out.

Selina didn't reply, simply closing the front door behind her as she left.

12

The End

KATE TOOK THE KIDS' CLOTHES OUT OF THE TUMBLE dryer and folded them. Laundry for the two boys was a never-ending job. Abigail often helped with the laundry, knowing that she caused some of the extra workload by changing the boys into outfits for various photoshoots destined for the internet. Of course, one of the boys would have sticky hands or end up spilling a drink on the new clothes, and they'd end up back in the wash.

It was coming up to eight o'clock. The boys were in bed asleep and Kate was looking forward to finishing up the laundry and curling up in bed with a book.

She'd borrowed a few romance books from Abigail and was enjoying reading again, even if they were all straight romance and she had to flip past the pages where the couple started to get amorous.

She'd always done so, even long before she realised that her interests lay elsewhere. It was strange to look back at all the very obvious signs. She'd never really liked male company, and kissing a man often sent a shiver up her spine. She'd always assumed that it was simple nerves. Something she'd get used to.

It wasn't until years later that she realised that she preferred women. Not until she was married to a control freak. The memory of Simon made her shudder so hard she dropped a sock. Even now, he held some phantom control over her, sneaking into her nightmares and staring her down.

She snatched the sock up off the floor just as Michael entered the room.

"Oh good, I caught you before you went to bed." He poked his head back into the kitchen and closed the door, trapping them both in the utility room.

Kate's heart started to beat a little faster. Michael seemed nice enough, but she didn't know him that well. In all the time she'd been working for Abigail, Michael had spent three quarters of that time working away from home. The remaining time he was either on the phone or in and out of the house like a yo-yo.

"Yes, I was about to head up." Kate quickly and half-heartedly folded the last couple of items.

"Selina is coming over shortly, she's dropping off some paperwork for Abi to sign. But I need a couple of moments with her to talk about some plans for Abi's birthday. I was wondering if you could keep Abi busy with something while we talk?"

Kate quickly nodded. "Yes, of course." She agreed in the hope that the door would be opened again and this awkward encounter would be over.

Michael didn't notice her discomfort. He folded his arms and leaned back against the washing machine. "It's weird, Selina's been over here more in the last month than she has in the past five years. Looks like the ice queen might be thawing in her old age." He laughed at his own joke.

Kate felt irritated by his comment. "I think it's nice that she's trying to make a connection with the boys."

Michael looked at her, a lopsided grin on his face. "You're quite a soft touch, aren't you?"

Kate shook her head and turned back to her laundry basket.

"I don't mean that as a bad thing, it's sweet."

Suddenly, she felt Michael standing right behind her. She didn't turn around because she knew if she did, they'd be face to face and much closer than she was happy with.

"Actually, I've been meaning to tell you," Michael said, his mouth much too close to her ear, "I think you're very lovely. A great addition to this family. We may not know each other that well, but I hope to change that… soon."

Kate's breath trapped in her throat. She had a couple of seconds to decide if Michael was being nice or, as she suspected, was trying to make a move on her. She wondered if she was being paranoid. There were always rumours about the father of the house and the nanny. The porn industry was practically built on it.

She ran his words over and over in her head. Was he being nice, or was he being a creep?

His fingers softly touched her upper arm.

She swallowed hard. Suddenly all the time away from home, the strange working hours, and the cryptic comments from Selina made sense. So did the fact that such a lovely family had gone through au pairs like tissues before Kate had arrived.

Michael wasn't the sweet father and husband he portrayed himself to be, and Kate wasn't about to go down that road. Her mind was made up.

She hurriedly stepped away from him, putting some much-needed space between them. From this safe distance, she glared at him. "Don't touch me. Don't ever touch me."

Michael's creepily pleasant smile vanished in an instant. Now he looked angry, defensive.

"As if I'd want to touch you," he spat back at her. "Some little nothing like you."

"Open the door." Kate nodded her head towards the closed door behind him. "I want to leave."

"Oh, you'll leave all right. You're fired. And if you tell Abi a single thing about what you *think* happened here, then I'll make sure it's the last thing you say."

Kate had heard enough. She shouldered her way past Michael and rushed to her room. She closed the door behind her, desperately wishing it had a lock.

Her brain swam in a foggy sea of panic. The only clear thought was that she had to get out of there. She had to leave. She looked out at the cold, dark night and then at her soft bed.

The thought of sleeping on the streets that evening was unappealing to say the least. A glance at the clock told her that she'd never get a bed at the shelter.

She had money, but she didn't want to waste it on a hotel. If she was soon to be homeless and unemployed, she'd need every penny she had to survive. Wasting large amounts of her small savings account on a hotel for the night was not in the cards.

She sucked in a few deep breaths, attempting to fight off the panic and calm herself down.

"I can stay tonight," she whispered to herself. "Leave in the morning."

The door flew open, cracking loudly against the wall.

Kate jumped, spun around, and found herself face to face with a furious Abigail.

"Get out," she growled.

Kate swallowed. "Let me explain—"

"You hit on my husband? Under my own roof? While I was in the next room?" Abigail's voice grew louder and louder. "You were my friend!"

Friend was a push. Kate was hired as a nanny to the boys but was given additional tasks in line with a maid. She cooked, cleaned, and did the laundry, but she'd done it all happily, relieved to be in a job and in a safe home. Abigail was kind to her, but they were not friends.

"I didn't do anything. He came onto me!" Kate explained.

Abigail scoffed, and Kate instantly realised that she could never win this particular battle of He Said, She Said. To Abigail, Michael was a saint. She adored her husband to the extent that his behaviour would never be in question.

Kate felt unsteady on her feet. She knew what was coming. Her topsy-turvy life was about to throw another serious curveball. Everything was about to change.

"Get out," Abigail repeated. "I don't ever want to see

you again. You have five minutes to get the hell out of my house."

"But—"

Abigail turned and ran down the hallway, the sound of her bedroom door cracking shut loudly behind her.

Kate sank to her knees, her hands shaking in her lap.

13

Missing

SELINA SLAMMED HER CAR DOOR SHUT. THE LAST thing she wanted to do was spend her evening filling in paperwork and speaking with her pathetic brother-in-law. Thankfully, it would be a short visit. She thought about the bottle of wine that was chilling in the fridge and mentally flipped through her music collection to find the best pairing.

A free evening at home was a rarity. Not that this was much of one, but she'd take a couple of hours wherever she could find them.

Before she could even get to the front door, it flew open.

Abi's face was red, her eyes swimming with tears. Selina would have been worried if she wasn't so adept at identifying her younger sister's moods.

This was the angry face. The face that first made an appearance when they were children and Selina had told her that she wasn't allowed in her room anymore. Barring Abi had been the only way she'd managed to get any peace and quiet when they were growing up. It hadn't gone down well with Abi. She'd been tears and tantrums.

Much like she looked now.

"Problem?" Selina asked, cutting straight to the point.

"That *woman*," Abi spat.

"Which one?" Selina started to remove her leather gloves, expecting to be invited into the house any moment now.

"That bitch. She, she was all over Michael. He had to fight her off!"

Selina was becoming frustrated by the blocked entrance and the riddles. Not to mention the fact that Michael was never to blame. She sighed. "Explain."

"Kate," Abi said.

"Kate?" Selina blinked. "Threw herself… at Michael?"

"Yes!"

Selina threw her head back and laughed. It was the most ridiculous thing she'd heard all day, and that included Margaret's request for a £10,000 wine budget.

Michael appeared in the hallway, looking over Abi's shoulder, as shifty as ever.

"Don't laugh!" Abi commanded her.

"But it's hilarious!" She pointed at Michael. "You're honestly telling me that sweet, pretty, young girl threw herself at that brain-dead, balding, flabby excuse for a human?"

"Selina!" Abi admonished.

Michael simply turned and walked away.

"That's preposterous," Selina continued. "Kate would never, ever do something like that."

She didn't know how she knew that, but she did.

Somehow her few interactions with Kate had left her in no doubt of the woman's integrity. Besides, she knew that Kate wouldn't risk her job and home over someone as sickening as Michael.

"She did."

"Did you see it?" Selina demanded. "Or did your oaf of a life partner tell you what happened?"

Abi stalled for a moment, and Selina rolled her eyes.

"You're so naïve. That man is sleeping his way across the country. Business trips? Were you born yesterday? I think it's far more likely that he's the one at fault here." Selina paused. "Where is she?"

She was suddenly aware of how cold it was standing on the driveway. A shiver ran up her spine at the thought of Kate not being in the relative safety of the house.

"Gone. I kicked her out." Abi jutted her chin up. "I didn't want her near my children."

Selina barked out a laugh. "If you really cared about bad influences on your children, you'd get a divorce." She turned around and stalked back to her car.

"Where are you going?" Abi asked.

"I have somewhere to be." Selina got into her Porsche and started the engine. She wasn't about to explain to her sister that she'd just thrown a homeless woman out into the streets on the word of her adulterous husband.

She reversed off the drive without a glance back at Abi. Her mind was full of questions. Where would Kate go? What was the address of the women's shelter? How long had she been gone?

On top of all of that, the biggest question of them all: why did she care?

Selina knew she wasn't in line for any good Samaritan award. Indeed, if there was an opposite of that, she'd be a shoe-in.

But she was operating on sheer instinct. Desperation raced through her veins alongside the adrenaline. She had to find Kate, had to know that she was okay.

She had no idea what she would do once she found her. That was a problem for later.

Selina put her mobile phone in the cradle, which synced it to her satnav system. Once it had connected, she asked her phone for a list of local women's shelters. After some trial and error, she managed to find the address of a place that looked most likely.

She looked at the clock. 21:02.

Trawling through her memory, she recalled that Kate had said something about availability being limited at the shelter she'd frequented. She might have mentioned a cut-off time, but Selina couldn't be certain.

She slammed her hand down on the steering wheel, cursing her lack of interest in other people when they spoke.

For a brief moment, she tried to think about what she would do if she were in Kate's position, but quickly shuttered that direction of enquiry. She had no idea what she would do. Luckily for her, she'd never been even close to being homeless. The whole concept of it being possible was foreign to her.

But it was a stark reality to Kate, and that worried Selina. She briefly analysed why she cared. Did she feel responsible? Abi had been the one to kick her out. Selina hadn't even been involved in her getting the job.

But she felt some kind of strange duty towards Kate. It mattered that she was okay.

Selina shook off the thought. She needed to focus on finding her.

She wondered if she would be able to convince Abi that she was being ridiculous and convince Kate to go back to her job. It was unlikely on both counts. Abi considered Michael to be the best husband and father on the planet. And why would Kate want to go back to live in a house with that terrible, harassing man?

She needed another solution, but she'd find that when she found Kate.

After a lot of driving around aimlessly, and consulting her satnav multiple times, she found the women's shelter. It was a run-down building next to a sex shop which she didn't know existed. "Ridiculous," she muttered. Whoever had chosen this location as the perfect spot for a women's shelter needed to answer some serious questions.

She stepped out of the car, pressing the lock button on her key fob multiple times just to be certain. After a deep breath, she stepped through the door and into the shelter.

A makeshift reception had been created by someone hacking a square hole in the wall between the hallway and an office. She peered in and made eye contact with a kind-looking woman in her sixties.

To say the woman looked surprised to see Selina in her Gucci suit would have been an understatement.

"I'm looking for someone," Selina explained. "Kate…" She trailed off, realising only then that she couldn't even remember Kate's full name.

The woman looked at her with suspicion. "We don't give out any details of our residents."

Selina quickly recognised that this would not be a battle won by force. She took a breath to calm herself.

"I can understand that; I just want to know if she's safe. She used to come here often, and I understand that she's suddenly found herself homeless again, through no fault of her own. I'm looking for her to make sure she doesn't end up on the streets tonight."

The warring emotions on the woman's face were clear. She had information to give but was evaluating Selina's sincerity.

"I don't need to see her, just to know if she is safe." She pulled her purse out from her handbag and plucked out some notes. "If she's here, please give her this. Maybe she can buy some food, a sleeping bag."

Selina didn't know what homeless people spent their money on. She'd always assumed it was drugs, but now she knew better.

The woman placed her hand over the stack of notes to keep Selina from adding to the pile. "I'm sorry, dear. She's not here. She came a while ago, but we're full."

Selina's breath caught. It had always been a possibility that Kate was out there somewhere, but it wasn't until now that she realised how terrifying that possibility was. For the first time that evening, she actually felt as if she had lost Kate. Which was true, she had no idea where Kate could be. Her one hope had just turned out to be a dead-end.

She dropped her purse back into her bag and turned to leave.

"Your money," the woman reminded her.

"Keep it. It's a donation," Selina called back.

She was in her car and driving before she realised that she should have asked the woman at the shelter where Kate might have gone. Surely, she'd know more about the local homeless population than Selina could guess.

She drove slowly through the various central streets in Parbrook: by the station, by the high street, and by her own building in case Kate was back in the car park. Her heart sank as each location turned up nothing. On top of that, it was dark, and she was finding it increasingly more difficult to see.

She spotted a couple of police officers on patrol and pulled up beside them.

"Excuse me," she called.

A male officer turned and approached the car.

"I'm looking for someone," Selina explained. "Long story, but she used to be homeless, then she wasn't, and tonight she is again. I know this sounds strange, but where do homeless people congregate?"

He tilted his head and looked at her thoughtfully before answering. "Wherever there is shelter. Store entrances, bridges, that kind of thing. You're a friend?" he asked.

Selina was beginning to realise how suspicious she must look, driving around the darkened streets in her Porsche looking for a homeless person.

"Yes, I'm sort of her guardian angel, but I dropped the ball," she admitted.

He looked at her for a few seconds. "Try the supermarket," he eventually suggested, presumably after considering her worthy of the advice.

She sighed in relief. "Thank you."

"Good luck. What's her name?"

"Kate. I… I don't know her full name."

"We'll keep an eye out for her. Can I take your contact details?"

Selina eagerly handed him her business card. "Thank you. Even if she doesn't want to see me, I'd like to know if she's okay."

He took the card and slipped it into one of the multiple utility pockets on his uniform. Both officers continued on their way, and Selina drove off towards the large supermarket in town.

She continued looking at every person as she drove. Suddenly, the small commuter town of Parbrook seemed enormous. Not that it was really that small. Just a lot smaller than London, where she and Addington's had been based ten years before.

The size of her task was not going to put her off. Selina lived for the impossible challenge. However, she did wish she had a little more information, that she had been a little more prepared for this particular hurdle.

Because this one mattered. Kate mattered.

She passed a familiar figure and quickly pulled the car over. She turned and looked out of the rear window to check if her eyes were playing tricks on her. They weren't.

Kate stood outside the doorway to a law firm, laying down a sleeping bag on the raised step. Selina felt an enormous weight lift from her.

She jumped out of the car and rushed towards Kate.

Kate obviously heard her heels and turned to look at her. She held up her free hand.

"No, no way. Just go away, Selina."

Selina paused. She supposed she should have been expecting that. She'd not exactly been a good omen for Kate. Nor had she been particularly pleasant to her.

"I just heard what happened. Well, I heard Abi's pathetic rendition of it and figured out the more likely scenario. I wanted to see if you're okay."

Kate stared at her in astonishment. "Yeah, I'm peachy." She dropped the sleeping bag onto the step and folded her arms. "How are you?"

"Sarcasm doesn't suit you," Selina replied. "Come on, let's go."

"Go?"

Selina was already turning and heading back to her car. She stopped, surprised that Kate wasn't already following her. She looked over her shoulder.

"Yes, let's go. You're not staying here."

A bubble of laughter erupted from Kate before she took a seat on the step and continued setting up her makeshift home.

Selina slowly turned around. She couldn't figure out what was happening. "I'm not taking you to Abi's—"

"You're not taking me anywhere," Kate interrupted. "You don't get to make decisions for me, Selina."

"You can't stay here."

"I can do whatever I like. You don't own me. You're not going to sweep in and make me forever beholden to you. I'm not *thanking* you, Selina."

"You're extremely stubborn."

"I am. It's all I have."

Selina noticed a man in the distance. He swayed uneasily and was walking towards them. She blew out a breath. She didn't have time to psychoanalyse whatever it was Kate was saying. There was an obvious solution. Kate just needed to hurry up and get with the program.

"We can discuss this later. Get in the car," Selina demanded.

"Why are you even here?" Kate asked.

"I'll explain once you get in the car."

"Am I not speaking English?" Kate asked. "Or are you so wrapped up in your own world that you naturally expect everyone to do exactly as you say? I'm not one of your employees."

"Please, get in the car," Selina gritted out.

"Better. But the answer is still no."

Selina nodded her head towards the clearly drunken man who was still approaching.

Kate turned to look at him and then looked back at Selina. She shrugged. "Seen worse," she said.

Selina couldn't believe how obstructive Kate was being. She didn't have time to figure out what was going on in her head, not with a probable troublemaker edging closer to them. She stalked forward and picked up the sleeping bag. Kate grabbed the other end, and they ended up in a ridiculous tug-of-war.

Selina dropped the sleeping bag in favour of a rucksack and carried the heavy bag towards her car.

"Selina!" Kate protested.

She pressed a button on her key fob, and the boot lid

sprung open. She put the rucksack in just as Kate reached in and pulled it out again.

"What do you want from me?" Selina demanded. "I've spent the last hour tracking you down. I just want to make sure you have a bed for the night. Not a doorway!"

"You can't just kidnap me from the street," Kate retaliated.

"I'm just trying to get you to see sense. Come with me. I'll take you to my place, I have a spare room. Or I'll pay for a hotel for you for the night. You don't even have to talk to me. Just… please." Selina felt suddenly exhausted. "Please."

She saw the drunken man stumbling towards them.

"Are you all right?" he asked Kate.

"She's fine," Selina said.

"Is she bothering you?" He gestured to Selina.

Selina rolled her eyes and looked at Kate. "Yes, am I bothering you?"

Kate looked at her thoughtfully for a moment. She raised her eyebrow. Selina rolled her eyes.

Kate turned to the man. "I'm fine. Thank you for checking on me, though."

"You sure?" He checked again.

She flashed him a smile. "Yeah, I'm all good. Thank you. Have a nice night."

He stared at Selina for a few seconds before he continued his way down the street.

Kate watched him go for a moment before turning back to Selina. "One night," she said. "I'll stay with you for one night. That's it."

Selina's heart soared. She quickly wiped the smile off

her face. "I should think so. I'm not a hotel," she mock-complained.

Kate chuckled. "You're an enormous pain in the arse, you know that, right?"

"I've been told," Selina admitted. "Get the rest of your things. I don't have all night."

Kate gave her an exasperated look before turning around and fetching her belongings from the doorway.

Selina smiled as soon as her back was turned. Kate would be safe that evening. And maybe Selina could figure out a way of convincing her to stay a little longer.

14

The Penthouse

Kate looked around Selina's apartment in awe. *Penthouse apartment*, she corrected herself. Because, of course, Selina would live in the most luxurious apartment in the whole town.

Parbrook wasn't much, just another commuter town on the outskirts of London, but even the smaller locations outside of London commanded enormous salaries for people to reside in them. Location was everything, and Selina had one of the best addresses in town. Just outside of the main areas, in an exclusive residential neighbourhood. There was a doorman and a concierge who greeted them upon arrival. The elevator displayed a lower level for a gym and a pool area.

"Your room is down the corridor, at the end on the right," Selina said. "There's a bathroom next door, which you can use exclusively. The master has an en suite." She kicked off her heels and put them away in a hallway closet which was the size of Kate's bedroom at Abigail's house.

It was becoming clear that the Porsche Selina drove

and the designer suits she wore were not for show. Selina really was extremely wealthy.

And that made Kate unreasonably angry.

She knew in her heart that Selina was not to blame for what had happened, but she couldn't forget that Selina had set her on the path. If she hadn't wanted to move Kate on from the car park, she never would have got her the job at Edge. If she hadn't been working at Edge when Selina's sister came in, she wouldn't have ended up working for her. She wouldn't have ended up trapped in a small utility room with a man she—

Most of all, she wouldn't have lost her place on the council waiting list for housing. Being a live-in nanny meant she'd happily removed her name. Now she'd be back to the end of the list, a list which kept changing on a daily basis as it was.

"Tea? Coffee?" Selina asked. "Have you eaten?"

Kate watched her walk into the apartment while she remained in the hallway, attempting to control her breathing. In a few short hours, her life had been turned upside down. It brought back bitter memories of a time she was desperate to forget.

Selina reappeared in the hallway, a look of confusion on her face. "Are you deaf?"

Any other day, Kate would have ignored Selina's rude comment, but today wasn't any other day. Today, Kate was angry and getting angrier by the second. Adrenaline pumped through her blood. Michael's behaviour and then Abigail's reaction played over and over again in her head.

"This is just another way for you to extract a thank you from me, isn't it? To play... what did you call yourself?" Kate furrowed her brow in thought, trying to recall how Selina had arrogantly introduced herself a few weeks previous. "Oh, yes, my guardian angel."

Selina interlocked her fingers in front of her and looked passively at Kate.

"It's all some game for you, isn't it?" she continued. "Living in your high-rise palace, looking down at the little people. Now and then you'll throw one of us a coin and expect us to bow down to you with gratitude. Does it kill you that I won't do that? Is that why you keep raising the bar? A coffee, a job, a home for the night? Just waiting for me to finally crack and tell you how *wonderful* you are?"

Selina waited for Kate to stop her rant before she gestured into the apartment.

"The kitchen is through there. Feel free to help yourself to anything in the fridge. The freezer is a little sparse, but you're welcome to anything you may find in there. Cupboards, too. Tea and coffee are in the cabinet above the kettle. You should be able to find anything without too much hassle. There's a utility area if you wish to wash or tumble dry anything."

Selina picked up her handbag from the table she'd placed it on. "Obviously, feel free to enjoy the television in the living room. You should have everything you need in the bathroom, but if you can't find something, then let me know. My room is through that hallway." She pointed. "I'm suddenly very tired, so I'll probably read in bed. I'll say good night now."

Selina turned and quickly moved towards the hallway she'd indicated.

Kate winced. She'd lashed out at someone who didn't

deserve it. Or maybe Selina did deserve it. She couldn't tell anymore. She lifted up her two bags and walked towards the guest room.

The apartment was tastefully decorated, not ostentatious as Kate had expected. Dark blues and light greys complimented each other to make the open-plan space cosy and welcoming. She looked longingly at the long corner sofa, two comfortable-looking tub chairs, a large flat-screen television, and shelves and shelves of books that filled the living area. If she had the money, this would be her dream room to relax in.

She pulled her gaze away and focused on finding the guestroom. The carpet of the hallway was thick and plush, and she felt like she was walking on marshmallow.

At the end of the hallway, she walked through the only doorway. She dumped her bags on the floor of the guestroom and looked around in awe. It looked like a luxury hotel suite, the kind she'd only ever seen before in photographs.

The king-size bed was beautiful in creams and browns, its pillows and scatter cushions piled perfectly. Two cabinets bookended the sumptuous bed, both with designer lamps and one with an iPod dock and clock. Original artwork adorned the walls, tasteful and modern.

The carpet in the guestroom was springier than the hallway, if that was possible. Kate wanted to kick off her shoes and socks and dig her toes into the fibres. She didn't, though; she didn't feel comfortable or safe to do so. Her heart was still thundering in her chest, and her fight-or-flight response was on red alert.

She looked out of the window and blew out a long breath.

She was angry at Selina, but it was misplaced anger. She was furious that Selina had succeeded, had a good job, a wonderful home, and a family who loved her. Kate would have been happy with one of those, but Selina had them all, and seemingly didn't appreciate a single one of them.

That's not fair, she chided herself. *You don't know her. Not really.*

She noticed something move out of the corner of her eye. She jumped, nearly letting out a scream, but she managed to stay silent when realisation hit her.

"Hi there!" Kate bent down and held out her hand to the cat who had appeared from behind the curtain.

The cat ignored her and continued its slow walk across the room.

Kate remained crouching, hand outstretched. "Here, kitty… come here, little kitty…"

The giant ball of fluff continued to meander away, completely ignoring her.

"About as rude as your owner, aren't you, little kitty?" Kate sighed.

"Her name is Missy."

Kate leapt to her feet, not having noticed Selina standing in the doorway.

"She's not rude, she's eighteen. Sadly, she's blind and deaf." Selina took a couple of steps into the room and picked up Missy. "I have no such excuse, I'm just rude. I just remembered that this is Missy's favourite place to hang out when I'm not in and thought I'd come and remove her. Good night."

She turned around to leave.

"Selina, wait."

She paused but kept her back to Kate.

"I'm sorry," Kate began. "I shouldn't have said that, and I shouldn't have said what I said before. It's just been a very, *very* hard evening."

"I imagine it has been. No offence taken; I've heard worse. Good night."

"Wait," Kate asked again.

Selina turned. She was holding Missy, and the giant fluff ball was leaning into her happily.

"I mean it. I'm sorry. I shouldn't have said what I did. You're… you're just an easy target," she admitted. "And I know you're strong enough to take it. But that doesn't mean it's right. So, I'm sorry. Really."

Selina regarded her for a few moments before giving a small incline of her head. "Apology accepted."

"Maybe we could have some coffee together?" Kate glanced at the clock on the bedside table. "Or some tea, as it's late. You can tell me all about Missy."

Selina looked like she was considering it. Kate hoped that she'd agree. She felt bad for sending her misdirected anger in Selina's direction. She wanted to ensure that her apology had been accepted, and to take her mind off the events of the evening. Sharing a hot drink and talking about an eighteen-year-old blind and deaf cat seemed as good a way as any to achieve that.

"Very well," Selina agreed. "Just don't get upset when I tell you that she was a stray I took in."

Kate laughed. "I see you have a type."

"Don't kid yourself. You don't look eighteen," Selina joked before leaving the room.

"I take it back, you *are* rude," Kate said as she followed her.

"Never said I wasn't," Selina replied.

15

Letting Her Go

THE EXHAUSTION HELPED SELINA TO SLEEP LIKE A log. But at five o'clock she snapped wide awake, with questions and half-formed plans swimming around in her head.

Last night, she and Kate had spoken for nearly an hour. Kate had steered the conversation into easy topics: the cat, the weather, even the state of politics in the country. Everything but the topics Selina wanted to discuss.

Selina hadn't pushed, which had surprised her. It wasn't common for her to leave questions unanswered, but there was something in Kate's mannerisms that told her that it wasn't the right time.

She also knew there was an invisible clock ticking over her head. Kate had reluctantly agreed to stay, but she was fairly sure that agreement wouldn't extend beyond one evening. And so, Selina was in a battle against time to fix things. Or attempt to, at least.

For some reason, it had become her number one priority to ensure that Kate was safe in a situation where she could get back on her feet and eventually flourish. Kate hadn't asked for her help. In fact, she'd actively tried to push Selina away, but she felt a pull towards righting wrongs.

Not that she knew exactly what those wrongs were, but she had some idea.

Regardless of her sister's denial, Selina knew that Michael was having affairs all the time. The young, attractive live-in nanny would be just his kind of conquest and was probably the reason Abi could never keep a nanny or an au pair in the house for more than a few months.

Whatever had happened between Kate and Michael had touched a nerve with Kate in a big way. Her usual confidence had slipped. During their late-night conversation, she seemed nervous, uncertain, and quick to anger. She'd lashed out at Selina before Selina had truly had the opportunity to say or do anything wrong.

She'd not known Kate for long, but this behaviour seemed very out of character.

She suspected she knew the reason; Kate had possibly been attacked in the past. Possibly in an abusive relationship. She knew not to make wild assumptions about things she didn't know, but she had a good nose for these things and was rarely wrong.

The thought left her feeling helpless and angry.

It was none of her business, but somehow their lives had intertwined enough times for Selina to feel like she couldn't ignore the matter.

She wasn't naïve enough to think that she could solve all of Kate's problems, but maybe she could help Kate get her life back together.

Which was why, at five-oh-seven, Selina had immediately got out of bed, showered, and started putting her plan into action.

By the time Kate came out of the guestroom at half past seven, Selina was feeling quietly pleased with herself.

"Good morning," she greeted her guest.

"Morning," Kate replied. "I'll be out of your hair shortly."

"Nonsense. Sit and have some breakfast. I'd like to talk to you."

Kate eyed Selina suspiciously. Her hair was casually tucked behind her ears, and she looked well-rested but tense. Selina hoped that she'd be able to convince Kate of her ideas, but that tension worried her. She sat up straight on the breakfast barstool and met Kate's gaze.

"Why do I get a strange sinking feeling?" Kate asked, pulling a mug out of the cupboard.

"Because you're a naturally pessimistic personality?"

"You're one to talk!" Kate laughed.

"I never said I was an optimist." Selina looked at her laptop and clicked open the email from her HR manager. As she suspected, everything was falling nicely into place.

"So, what do you want to talk about?" Kate asked after pouring herself a mug of coffee.

"Have some toast. Or cereal," Selina ordered. Kate seemed to be in a listening mood, and Selina wanted to ensure she got some food inside her before the potential backlash emerged. Kate wasn't one to accept help lightly, and Selina knew herself well enough to know she wasn't good at offering it in a sensitive manner.

Kate rolled her eyes and started to pour some cereal

into a bowl. She splashed some milk on top before making a show of eating a spoonful.

"I've secured you a job," Selina said, taking advantage of a full mouth to not get any reply.

Kate's eyes widened.

"At my company," Selina continued.

Her eyes widened impossibly further. She chewed faster in order to be able to speak, most likely in disagreement.

"Not working for me," Selina reassured.

"Who'd you bribe this time?" Kate asked a split second after swallowing.

"No one. I looked at the list of vacant positions and found one that you could do, which needed to be filled. You're doing the company a favour by taking the role without us having to hire an agency to fill the gap."

Kate looked unsure. "What job?"

"A role in the post room. Sending out letters, delivering post to the various departments in the building. It's not glamorous, but it's safe, secure, and pays better than Abi ever would."

Selina turned her laptop around and gestured for Kate to look at the screen. "This is the email from the HR manager; the job is yours if you want it. You'll have a contract; the salary is listed. And I didn't have to fire anyone, I promise," she reassured her. "In fact, you don't have to see me at all. You can hand my post to my assistant. Our paths need never cross, if that's what you wish."

"Isn't she on maternity leave soon?" Kate asked while reading the email.

"Oh, yes." She'd forgotten about the rather large problem directly in her future. Something to think about. "But whoever ends up taking the role—"

"Not me."

"No, not you," Selina said. "You can leave the post with them if you don't want to see me."

"It's not that I don't want to see you," Kate explained. "I just don't want to be beholden to you. I don't want you to feel like you own me, or for me to feel like I owe you. Although, I do feel like I owe you already."

"Well, you don't."

Kate turned to look at her. "But I do. Saying that I shouldn't won't make me change the way I feel."

Selina shrugged. "Fine, feel however you wish. But you don't owe me anything." She stood up and took her empty coffee mug to the dishwasher. "Of course, you're welcome to stay here until you get a place of your own."

"No, I can't do that."

Selina paused as she put her mug on the rack. She'd worried that would be Kate's answer. She'd agonised about the best way to help keep her safe. Her knee-jerk reaction was to give her all the money she needed, rent an apartment on her behalf, or force the woman to live with her, but she knew that Kate would react badly to any of those suggestions.

It was time to tread lightly.

"I'll take the job, and I'll stay at the shelter for now. Once I save enough money, I'll get a place of my own," Kate said.

Selina kept her back to her, pretending to rearrange

the three items in the dishwasher. She didn't want Kate to see the disappointment on her face.

The evening before had been a shock for Selina. She'd somehow gone from wanting Kate gone from her business car park at any cost, to being horrified at the thought of the woman out on the cold streets at night.

Last night she'd hovered on the edge of panic, knowing full well that she would have searched every square inch of Parbrook until she'd located Kate. Even if it had taken her all night.

"I appreciate your offer, it's very kind of you," Kate added, obviously assuming Selina's silence was steeped in anger.

She stood up and faced Kate, plastering a smile onto her face as she did. "Of course, I understand. The offer is there, but you have to do what you feel is right for you." She looked at her watch. "I'm planning to do some work from home and then go into the office late. If you want to shower and get ready, we can go in together at, say, eleven?"

"Are you sure you didn't bribe someone to get me the job?" Kate joked.

"Don't ask questions you won't like the answer to." Selina winked. She turned and started to walk towards her bedroom.

"Selina?!" Kate shouted.

"Of course I didn't. I learn from my mistakes!" Selina called back. She entered her bedroom and closed the door behind her.

Selina wasn't skilled in this kind of situation. Her job involved her identifying a problem and putting all possible resources into fixing that problem as quickly as possible. That simply wasn't possible with Kate. Kate was fiercely independent and strong-willed. Maddeningly so.

She'd tossed a variety of ideas over in her mind all morning. She kept coming back to the same thing: in order to help Kate, she needed to allow her the freedom to grow and develop on her own.

Selina needed to respect that.

Even if she hated it.

16

A Casual Lifeline

"How are you with computers?"

"I'm good with them," Kate replied.

Ivor Robinson's face beamed at the news. He was the manager of the post room of Nicholas Addington and Sons and was well over retirement age. If Kate were to guess, the tiny man in front of her was undoubtedly in his seventies.

He wore a suit and a tie, despite the other six members of the post room staff all wearing casual clothes. His thinning grey hair was slicked back, and he wore thick glasses. He looked like a kindly grandfather figure, and everyone she'd met so far in the post room seemed to like and respect him.

She'd driven in with Selina that morning and was quickly introduced to the HR manager who took her through some standard paperwork. Within an hour she was in the post room being introduced to her new work colleagues.

It was a bit disorientating considering just six hours

ago she had lain awake in bed thinking that she would soon be back on the streets with no prospects.

Now, suddenly, she was working in an office. She'd wanted to decline Selina's offer, but it was too good an opportunity to pass up. Kate wanted to be in control of her own destiny, but she recognised when it was time to accept a little assistance. Even if it did come from Selina.

It had been almost two months since she'd first encountered Selina. At first, Kate had been certain that she had a good grasp on the woman's personality. Now, she wasn't so sure. Selina could be cold, harsh, determined, and ruthless, but Kate was beginning to realise there was a lot more to her. Not that Selina made it easy.

"That's wonderful," Ivor said, waking her from her analysis. He leaned in close. "I've never really got on with them."

"They are tricky to master," Kate agreed. "Luckily, I grew up with them."

Ivor leaned back in his worn office chair and nodded.

"I bet that helps a lot. When I was at Royal Mail, we didn't have computers. So, I never learnt!" He chuckled to himself.

Kate tried to control her facial expressions at the shocking news that whenever Ivor had worked at the country's postal distribution network, there were no computers. Either Royal Mail were very slow on picking up technology, or Ivor had worked there a very long time ago.

Ivor gestured to his desk, which was cluttered with stacks and stacks of paper files, scraps of paper, pens, and the morning newspaper.

"I write whatever I want to email to people, and Clara sends it for me," he explained.

Kate blinked.

At that moment, Clara appeared with a piece of paper in her hand. Clara was a woman in her fifties who sat on the other side of the large room. When they had been introduced, Clara had seemed pleasant though quiet. Kate got the impression that Clara enjoyed being on her own, and wanted only minimal interaction with those around her.

"An email just came in, Ivor." She handed it to him.

"Right, let's see what they are saying now." Ivor reached forward and put on a pair of glasses. He held the piece of paper at arm's length and muttered to himself as he read the text.

Kate was close enough to him, and the paper was held out far enough, that she could easily see the printout. She read the contents of the message, and the one below, and quickly concluded that the top message was from someone who had mistakenly clicked reply to all, rather than just replying to person who had sent out the first message.

"What's she mean?" Ivor asked. "This doesn't make any sense!"

Kate sat quietly and waited for Clara to explain.

"I don't know," Clara said. "What should I reply?"

Ivor placed the paper on a spare corner of his desk and grabbed a pen. "I don't… know… what you… mean," he mumbled as he handwrote his reply.

Kate couldn't take it anymore. She gently put her hand on Ivor's to stop him from writing. "I think Susan has accidentally replied to all people on the email," she said.

Ivor's brow rose in confusion.

"When David sent the first message, he sent it to a mailing list, which you're on. There might be ten, or even a hundred people on that mailing list. But Susan has replied to everyone, rather than just David. I think this is a message for David only. You can ignore it."

Ivor read the letter again. And then again. After a moment he nodded. "Yes, because this doesn't make any sense." He turned to Clara and handed her the printed email. "Shred this. And then print out a fresh one and put it in the cabinet."

The phone on Ivor's desk rang.

"Excuse me a minute," he said to Kate before answering the call.

Kate nodded distractedly, too intent on watching Clara. Clara walked to the corner of the room and put the piece of paper into a shredder. She then returned to her computer and pressed a few buttons. She walked over to the printer and retrieved a piece of paper before finally crossing to a long row of filing cabinets and putting the paper in one of the drawers.

They're printing out and filing emails, Kate thought in amusement. She stared at the row of cabinets. *All the emails.*

She couldn't believe that the post room was operating forty years out of sync with the rest of the building. She'd seen some of the office space when the HR manager had shown her round. Everyone else was using state-of-the-art laptops. She even saw some tablets. But somehow, the basement was stuck in its own little time period.

Selina would implode if she knew about this, Kate thought.

Ivor put the phone down. "Sorry about that, my dear. Busy, busy."

"That's fine," Kate said. "I imagine you get a lot of calls."

As you don't have a computer on your desk, or know how emails work, she mentally added.

"I do!" he agreed. He stood up, bringing him to a height only a little taller than he'd been when sitting down. "Now, let's get you started."

———

Clara held the package in both her hands and visibly swallowed as she stared at the address label.

"Is everything okay?" Kate asked.

Clara was sweet but a little odd. Kate had quickly learnt that everyone in the post room was lovely but a little odd. Ivor had managed to put together a group of delightful misfits, and Kate was already falling in love with all of them.

"It's for Miss Hale." Clara looked at her, fear in her eyes.

"Miss Hale?"

"Selina Hale, the operations director. She's really mean. She fires everyone all the time."

Kate wondered if she should tell Clara that she knew Selina and risk rocking the boat with her new co-workers. She was pretty sure that no one would want to talk to her if they knew she was on speaking terms with

Selina. It had only been a couple of hours, and she didn't relish the idea of alienating her new colleagues so quickly.

"What's going on here?" Ivor was on his way, having seen the colour drain from Clara's face.

Clara held up the box. "It's for Miss Hale."

Ivor smile and looked at Kate. "I think Kate can take that. Apparently, she already knows Selina, don't you, my dear?"

"A little. Sort of," Kate confessed.

Clara quickly handed the package to Kate, a look of relief on her face. "Then Kate can always take Miss Hale's deliveries?" she asked Ivor eagerly.

"Yes, I think she can." Ivor looked at Kate for confirmation.

"Sure. I'll take this one up now." Kate pointed towards the corridor and the elevators.

"You remember the way?" Clara asked.

Kate nodded. "Sure, I'll be back in a couple of minutes."

Relief washed over her. Clara was so happy that she no longer had to deliver anything to Selina that she didn't seem to care that Kate knew Selina personally. She wondered if the conversation would reappear at a later date, once her colleagues had gotten to know her better.

She didn't know how she'd describe her relationship with Selina. They weren't friends. Not co-workers. Not really anything that could be easily described.

Kate pressed the elevator button for the twelfth floor.

She'd been surprised to realise that she'd had to hold herself back from defending Selina to Clara. Even though

Kate categorically agreed that Selina was mean, she'd still wanted to jump to her defence.

"She's rude," Kate reminded herself. "Don't be fooled by her."

Selina had been kind to her, but Kate wasn't ready to fully trust her yet. She'd met plenty of nice people who had turned out to only be willing to help her as long as it suited them. After a while, being a good Samaritan became boring or hard work, and most people drifted away.

She was determined to not be hurt anymore, and to do that, she had to remain tough.

She stepped out onto the twelfth floor and walked towards Selina's corner office. Kate stopped outside the office when she noted that Selina's assistant wasn't at her desk. She looked up and saw Selina walking around her office on the phone. She wondered if she should put the package on the desk and leave.

As she was pondering, Selina noticed her and waved her in through the glass window.

Kate sighed in relief that the question had been answered and walked into Selina's office. She placed the box on Selina's desk, but before she could turn to leave, Selina gestured for her to wait.

Kate stood quietly as the operations director shouldered the phone, taking out a sharp-looking letter opener and efficiently slicing open the package.

"Well, of course we need to ensure that we stay on track. But at what cost?" Selina asked the person on the line. She placed the letter opener on the desk and opened the box. Kate didn't know why Selina had asked her to stay if she was insisting on remaining on her call. Her eyes started to wander around the room.

"Here."

She looked back at Selina who was holding out the contents of the package for her.

Kate hesitantly took the box.

Selina covered the mouthpiece of the phone. "It's cheap, so I doubt it will be much of a theft risk."

It was a mobile phone. Kate looked at Selina in confusion.

Selina handed her a Post-It note. "My personal number. There's credit on the phone. I understand the shelter gets busy. If you find yourself without a bed for the night, call me."

Kate's shaky hand took the note.

Selina took her hand from the mouthpiece. "That's quite frankly the most ridiculous thing I've heard in my life, Dominic. What business school did you go to again? I'll be sure to donate to them immediately to ensure no more graduates enter the business world so poorly prepared." She turned and continued her phone call.

Kate couldn't believe that Selina had been so casual about giving her what was essentially a lifeline. And had taken the time to choose a phone that wouldn't be a theft risk.

She felt tears welling in her eyes but refused to show them. She took a couple of deep breaths to calm herself down again.

It was the nicest thing that anyone had ever done for her in longer than she could remember. Selina had given her blanket permission to reach out if she needed help.

That was different to other people who hadn't even been there for her when the worst had already happened.

Kate didn't know if she'd ever actually call Selina, but the offer was incredible. She looked at Selina, who was thoroughly distracted by her call.

Maybe I got her wrong. Maybe she is a nice person under all this bluster, Kate thought. She turned to leave.

"Kate, one moment."

She looked back at Selina who was again covering the mouthpiece of the receiver. "When you're delivering post to marketing, could you see if you could accidentally over-hear what they are doing about the brokerage event? And then report back?"

Kate laughed louder than she had intended. Selina gave and Selina took away just as quickly.

"No, I won't spy for you," she said with a wide grin. "But thanks for the phone."

"Useless," Selina whispered good-naturedly before rolling her eyes and returning to her call.

17

A Heart of Ice

SELINA SLAMMED THE PHONE DOWN AND PUT HER head in her hands. Why people insisted on being incompetent was completely beyond her. It sometimes seemed like she was surrounded by idiots.

"Selina?"

She peeked up at Gemma who stood in the doorway to the office. She blinked a couple of times, realising that Gemma almost filled the doorway these days. It wouldn't be long now before the woman exploded or gave birth. It could literally be either given the tremendous size of her.

When did that happen? she wondered.

She hadn't been paying attention lately. Days were flying by with problem after problem, and she hadn't taken a moment to look at anything other than her cluttered desktop.

"I have that doctor's appointment to get to," Gemma reminded her.

"Oh, yes." Selina looked at the clock on the wall. *Where did the day go?*

"So, I'll see you tomorrow."

"Yes, good luck." Selina fixed a smile on her face as Gemma waved her goodbye and left the office.

As soon as she was gone, Selina put her head in her hands again and breathed out a long sigh. Gemma's replacement wasn't something that had found its way to the top of her to-do list just yet. She knew it was becoming an urgent issue, but so was everything else.

There were reports due, presentations to write and give, meetings to organise, budgets to restructure. Everything had come at once, and Selina was feeling the pressure.

But she knew it would all be worth it. Everything she was working on was high profile. Her seat in the board-room and her office on the thirteenth floor were all but guaranteed.

If she survived that long, she thought bleakly. She didn't even know what day it was. In some ways she hoped for a weekend arriving shortly, in others the thought of two days' lost productivity gave her shivers.

"Are you okay?"

She looked up. Kate had stepped into her office and was placing a handful of letters in her in-tray.

"Yes, I'm fine." Selina blew out a breath and dragged her laptop closer. She needed to see if accounts had finally done what she'd asked them to do one hundred times before.

She realised Kate still stood in front of her desk. She met Kate's eyes and raised her brow.

"You don't look fine," Kate replied. "What's up?"

Selina's hands stilled over the keyboard. She couldn't

remember the last time someone had genuinely enquired about her health.

"I'm just busy," she explained. "Lots of things happening at once. I'll get through it, and then things will look brighter."

She leaned back in her chair and regarded Kate with a smile. Kate just looked at her, clearly not believing a word she said. She took the opportunity to look at Kate. She was looking better than she'd ever seen her. There was a healthy glow to her skin, and she'd put on a little weight, which had been much needed. She seemed… happy.

"And how are you? Settling into the dungeon?" Selina asked, hoping to change the subject.

"It's been a month, I'm part of the furniture now. And you can stop calling it the dungeon. I'll accept basement."

"Very well, a reasonable trade. Life in the basement treating you well?"

"Yeah. Ivor's…" Kate trailed off as she looked for the appropriate word.

"Ivor," Selina supplied. The man was beyond ordinary descriptors.

"Yes. Exactly. He's a sweetheart. Bonkers, but sweet."

"I hear stories," Selina admitted. "Not from you, of course. You're apparently above spying for me." She recalled the few vague attempts she had made to extract information from Kate, only to be met with a laugh and a declaration that she was wasting her time.

"Clara got locked in a mail crate this morning," Kate said.

She gawked. "How is that even possible?"

Kate shrugged. "They're an impressive bunch. I'm surprised you haven't fired us all and installed robots."

"The thought crossed my mind, but Ivor is over seventy and has no idea what salary he should be paid for his role. I think he's still pre-decimal. I give him a farthing every other week and he's happy."

Kate laughed. "I don't believe it; I think you have a soft spot for him. For all of them. You can't bring yourself to force lovely little Ivor into retirement."

Selina let out a sad sigh. "I'm sorry to burst your bubble, but no, I'm not that kind-hearted. If I thought he was bad at his job, I'd fire him in a heartbeat. In fact, I've heard stories of the insanity that happens down in the post room, and I have considered investigating to see if a shake-up is needed. The only reason I haven't done so is because the department hires low-salaried staff, and it's not a good use of my time. Yet."

Kate's face fell.

Selina felt guilty for not living up to the ice queen with a secret heart of gold persona that Kate had obviously carved out for her.

"I'm sorry, I wish I could accommodate your dream of me having just a hard exterior and being a human being underneath it all, but I'm not. I'm the operations director. I'm the one who makes the hard choices."

Kate nodded her head and took a small step back. "I know. Just… don't work too hard. Take a break now and then," she requested before she left the office.

Selina watched her walk away. The young woman smiled and greeted people as she walked through the open-plan office. It was nice to see that she had settled into the company.

She'd seen Kate sparingly around the office but had not spoken to her often. She wondered if Kate had managed to find shelter every night, or if she had simply chosen not to use the phone she had given her.

Or if she had used it, but not to call Selina.

It was possible, maybe even probable. Selina didn't think she was the first person Kate would turn to in case of trouble, even if she wished she were.

She shook her head, having no idea where thoughts like that came from.

"Get back to work," she muttered to herself. "Let's get something finished today."

18

Stuck in the Middle

Kate pushed the post trolley through the eleventh floor, dropping off envelopes and packages as she went. It had been a few weeks, and she already felt like she could do her job in her sleep.

In fact, she wasn't entirely convinced that she hadn't sometimes done the deliveries while at least half asleep.

Everyone was lovely, both her colleagues in the post room and the people she met throughout the office. And, of course, she was very happy and grateful to have a secure, full-time job.

But to say she was bored would be an understatement.

She had no intention of rocking the boat. She was earning money during the day and able to get to the shelter each night. Life was good. She also knew that with just a couple more payslips in her account, she'd finally have the sum she needed to rent a room somewhere.

Parbrook was expensive, and commuting was even more expensive. So, for now at least, she was stuck at the shelter. Maybe one day in the future she'd have enough for her own apartment.

She finished her last delivery on the eleventh floor and made her way to the elevator. As she waited for the elevator to arrive, she wondered about the eager butterflies that bounced around her stomach each day when she entered the twelfth floor. There was something about the twelfth floor. It may have been because it was the second-to-last floor, or maybe because Selina Hale was based there.

Can't be, she told herself. *I rarely see her.*

Most times Kate only caught glimpses of Selina in her office as she handed the post to Gemma. Sometimes the office was empty, and Kate did her best to ignore the empty feeling that welled up inside her.

Now and then, Gemma was away from her desk and Selina was in. Kate usually took the opportunity to go into Selina's office and speak with her for a few minutes. Technically, she could leave the post in Gemma's in-tray but told Selina that she'd been instructed to not leave post unattended. This was not entirely true.

She pushed the trolley onto the twelfth floor and was ridiculously pleased to see Gemma standing in the corridor taking a phone call. A personal one, if she wasn't mistaken.

It wasn't the first time she'd caught Gemma sneaking away from her desk for personal reasons. Based on what she had learnt about Selina, it was quite a risk to take.

Kate nodded politely at Gemma as she passed by.

She wondered why Selina hadn't fired Gemma yet. She hated to admit it, but she could now see what Selina was talking about when she said that Gemma was all-consumed with her pregnancy and had no interest at all in her work.

Having a job that involved walking around the building meant that Kate easily spotted people who were away from their desks. Terry from corporate finance was always "stretching his legs". Jeanne was another person who spent more time chatting to people than at her own desk, and Gemma was forever on the phone in a corridor somewhere.

Kate couldn't understand why people took such risks, especially when someone like Selina would fire them in a heartbeat.

She rounded the corner and came to a stop.

There was a woman in Selina's office. She looked like she shouldn't be there. She had her coat on and a bag slung over her shoulder as if she had just walked in from outside. Then she realised that Selina was standing before her, and the two women were… arguing?

Without thinking, Kate abandoned the trolley and rushed into Selina's office in case something was amiss.

"I can't believe you just marched in here. Security should have thrown you out!" Selina was shouting.

Kate blinked. She'd never heard Selina raise her voice. Selina never needed to. She was terrifying enough without requiring any additional volume.

The intruder was maybe in her late forties and had long, dark brown hair. She wore glasses and had a kind expression.

"I wouldn't be here if you replied to any of my texts,

calls, letters, or any of my solicitors' texts, call, or letters. We are still technically married, you know."

Kate felt the air leave her lungs. This was the ex-wife. *Carrie*, she reminded herself.

"I can't even hear you." Selina sat down at her desk, dragged her laptop closer, and focused on the screen.

"Selina, we need to talk," Carrie said.

Selina completely blocked her out.

Carrie huffed and shook her head. "You're honestly like a child. I have no idea how I stayed married to you for so long."

Selina didn't reply. She continued to work as if no one were there.

Carrie turned to Kate and smiled. "Hi, I'm Carrie Lane." She held out her hand politely.

Kate shook her hand. "Hey, I'm Kate Morgan."

"Are you from security?" Carrie asked.

"No, post room. Just happened to be passing."

Carrie grinned. "Post room? In that case, would you mind passing on a message for me?" She nodded her head playfully towards Selina.

Kate smiled. "I can try."

"Could you please tell Selina that I am only requesting that she signs paperwork in order to release me from the apartment and our joint business. I don't want a part of either."

Kate looked at Selina, knowing full well that she had heard every single word. Selina didn't move an inch.

"Selina?" she asked.

Selina blinked and looked up. "Oh, hello, Kate. How can I help you?"

Is she really going to do this? Kate wondered before remembering who she was dealing with. Of course, Selina was going to be as obnoxious and difficult as possible.

"Carrie said that she wants you to sign paperwork to release her from the apartment and your joint business. She doesn't want a part of either," Kate repeated.

Selina chuckled as if Kate was some poor innocent with no idea of the way the world worked. "Kate, be a dear and please tell Carrie that I have no intention of signing that agreement because I'm fully aware that she really wants a portion of the pension fund that she insisted I set up."

She turned her focus back to her laptop.

Kate sighed and turned to Carrie, who said, "Tell her that I am legally entitled to a portion of that pension, and she was the one who set it up. Besides, I don't want it. I just want this to be over."

Kate nodded and turned to Selina. "You heard that, right?"

Selina carried on typing. "Heard what?"

"You're difficult to like, you know," Kate said. "Carrie said that she doesn't want the pension. She just wants this to be over."

"Please inform Carrie that the very first document she sent me demanded half of my pension and a good third of the savings account. I wasn't born yesterday."

Carrie snorted a laugh. "Truer words were never spoken."

"I wasn't born yesterday," Selina repeated, louder this time. "I know that entering into discussion will only lead to Carrie's rottweiler of a solicitor picking over my dead carcass."

Carrie was shaking her head. "Tell her…" She paused. "I'm sorry, Kate, was it?"

Kate nodded.

"I'm sorry, we shouldn't be putting you into the middle of this. We are grown women, I promise." Carrie turned to Selina. "That letter was a mistake. It hadn't been agreed to by me. I explained this to you time and time again. I don't want anything; I just want to be free of this. You must want that, too."

Selina typed slowly, obviously hearing but ignoring everything around her.

Carrie's shoulders sagged. "If you don't start talking to me, I'll have to take this further. I don't want to do that, but I can't live in this limbo any longer."

Selina's attention was fully turned to her laptop. It was clear that no one was going to get through to her now.

Carrie turned and looked at Kate. "Again, I'm sorry, that was very childish of us. You're not our personal peacekeeper."

Kate shrugged. "It's okay. I used to work on a mediation helpline, so I've dealt with much worse."

Carrie's eyes shone with interest. "A helpline?"

"Yes, it was a charity. We dealt with calls from people who were having trouble with their landlords or their employers. We'd sometimes be on calls for both sides to act as mediators."

Carrie was smiling and nodding. "Wonderful, that's just wonderful. So, how did you end up here?"

Kate ran a nervous hand through her hair. "Well, I…

long story short, my life kind of unravelled and I ended up homeless. I was homeless for about a year until I met Selina and she helped me, and I ended up here."

Carrie grinned knowingly and glanced at Selina. "Did she now?"

"Yes, she's got a heart of gold, whether she wants to admit it or not," Kate said a little defensively.

"I couldn't agree more," Carrie said. "Look, I know this isn't the time or the place, but I run a council-led initiative to help older citizens not feel so alone. We're desperately seeking a senior call operator. Would you be interested in applying for something like that? We've been interviewing for months and we can't find anyone who fits the bill, but I think you just might."

Kate looked at Carrie in shock. "Um. I…"

"You should apply," Selina said softly, without looking up.

Kate snapped her head towards Selina.

Is she angry at me? Does she want me gone? Kate worried.

She'd only stepped in to defend Selina from the stranger she'd spotted in her office. Somehow, she'd gotten herself more deeply involved in Selina's life. She wondered if Selina regretted that.

At the continued silence, Selina glanced up. "It's bound to be a better-paid position," she said, "and is much more suited to your experience and will therefore give you a chance at professional development and a career path."

Kate breathed again. She was ecstatic that Selina wasn't angry at her. In fact, Selina was again putting her first.

"I don't know," she admitted. "I haven't been here for long. I—"

"Don't think about the firm. Think about what is best for *you,*" Selina insisted. She pointed a pen at Carrie. "She's a relatively decent employer, and the council pay them well so it's a secure job. Surely more interesting than what you're doing now. I'd recommend you consider it. Carrie, I will call you this evening. Now, both of you, *get out.*"

The last two words were ground out with such venom that they didn't need telling again. They quickly left the office, Kate closing the door behind them.

"I know this isn't a conventional way to job-hunt," Carrie said, "but I'd love to speak with you more about this role."

Kate wasn't sure. Leaving the safety of Addington's and her team of misfits in the post room seemed liked a huge deal. Then again, she didn't know if she could take many more weeks of pushing the trolley around the building, watching Clara filing printed emails, or seeing Ivor handwrite replies to spam emails from Nigerian princes.

"How long did you work on your helpline?"

Kate thought back. It felt like multiple lifetimes ago, but, in reality, it had only been a few years.

"I was there for about three years, started out as a part-time volunteer. Then I got asked to take a permanent role after... I think about three months."

"And you liked the work?" Carrie asked.

Kate smiled at the memories. "Yeah, it was a great job. I mean, it was hard. Very hard. But the team and the job itself were great. No two days were the same, and you slept well knowing you'd made a difference."

Carrie was grinning from ear to ear. She pulled a business card out of her bag and handed it to Kate. "*Please* call me. I'd love to tell you more about us and hear more about you, just a casual chat. We'll see if we're a good fit. But I already have a great feeling about this," she said.

Kate looked at the card. Carrie was the chief executive. *The big cheese,* she thought to herself. She turned and looked through the glass partition at the other big cheese she knew.

"I don't want to let Selina down. She got me this job," Kate explained.

"They'll manage. And she just said that you need to look out for you, which is damned good advice." Carrie looked at Selina and shook her head as she started to button up her jacket. "She's also quite likely to call security, so I'm going to go before I anger her. Seriously, call me and we can arrange a chat."

Carrie disappeared into the corridor, and Kate looked down at the business card in her hand. It seemed like a good idea, but she was frightened of losing what she had.

This seemed to be a constant theme of her life lately, jumping from job to job. Kate's natural instinct was to hold on tight and not rock the boat. She knew how quickly everything could fall away.

"Call her."

Kate jumped. Selina had opened her office door and was now standing in the doorway with her arms folded and a steely expression etched on her face.

"I loathe her, but that's no reason for you to. A senior

role will pay well. You're clearly qualified. She's…" Selina swallowed uncomfortably. "She's a good person. Well, she is to her staff. Call her."

She took a step back and slammed the door closed.

"Thanks," Kate muttered to the closed door. "I think I will."

19

On the Move

"No... no... no... and absolutely not." Selina handed the stack of CVs back to the HR minion. "None of these are any good. Find more."

"But—"

"Now." Selina pointed to her office door.

The minion looked at her fearfully before nodding and hurrying away.

Selina rolled her eyes. Surely it wasn't this hard to find a temporary assistant. The HR department was acting as if it were akin to climbing Everest. She'd yet to even let someone through to the interview stage.

Everyone they suggested was either far too young with no experience, or far too old with the wrong kind of experience. She looked at Gemma through the glass partition. Gemma was shovelling pieces of chocolate into her mouth as if the expiry date were minutes away.

"Surely it can't be hard to replace *that*," she muttered to herself. Looking for a temporary replacement was still the least of her worries. Clients were leaving, profits were down, and Margaret was still planning an event on the scale of Sir Elton John's birthday. Not a day went by without Selina having to veto a ridiculous amount of money which Margaret had somehow pushed past a weak board member.

Selina was aware she'd come through the other side of these setbacks soon enough, she always did. She'd dealt with worse and always ended up on top. A firm hand and an eye for detail got you a long way in her line of business, and Selina knew she was the best.

But it was a time for vigilance and extra hours.

Which were exhausting, even though she knew it would be worth it when she single-handedly saved the company and increased profit margins yet again. The thirteenth floor beckoned. Jonathan Addington had all but told her which one of the two empty offices would be hers.

He was visiting every other day now, in between client lunches and golfing sessions, asking for an update and complaining about the fact that his bonus was currently looking a little slim.

While she enjoyed the fact that he needed her, she'd also like a break from having to explain basic concepts to him.

Gemma hurriedly hid her chocolate, and Selina noticed Kate push the trolley in front of Gemma's desk. They started talking, Gemma gesturing to her swollen belly and Kate grinning.

Selina had heard through the grapevine that Kate had accepted the job with Carrie. While she was unhappy that the post room's efficiency would no doubt take a nosedive, she was happy that Kate was doing well.

The post room job had only ever been temporary, a safe place for Kate to get back into the working environment while Selina kept an eye on proceedings from afar. She was pleased that Kate had built up her confidence enough to apply for and accept a new role. It was an essential step for Kate to rebuild her life.

Kate gestured towards Selina's door, so she quickly snatched up her pen and pretended she hadn't been watching them both.

There was a knock on the doorframe and then the sound of footsteps as Kate invited herself in and stood in front of Selina's desk.

"Hey," she greeted.

Selina looked up and acted surprised at who was stood in front of her.

"Good afternoon," she returned.

"It's time for me to say goodbye," Kate said.

Selina swallowed. For some reason she didn't want to say goodbye. Knowing that Kate was somewhere in the building at all times had been a little like a security blanket for her. She'd lost count of the number of weeks which had passed since that dreadful night she had anxiously searched the streets for Kate. It was still a permanent feature of her nightmares, only soothed by the knowledge that she knew Kate was safe and just a few floors away.

All the same…

"Thank you for all your hard work," Selina said formally.

"Thank you for the opportunity. And for pushing me to call Carrie. You were right, I needed to look out for myself. This new job is back to doing something that matters, and I'd forgotten what that felt like. And Carrie's helped me find an apartment. It's a council outreach project that I didn't know about, but it means that tomorrow I'll officially have a place of my own."

Excitement radiated from Kate, and Selina had to do her best to not get caught up in it.

"That really is wonderful news," she said. "I'm very happy for you."

"Brace yourself," Kate said with a grin, "because you're finally going to get that thank you that you wanted so badly all those months ago."

Selina smiled, lowered her pen, and rested comfortably in her chair. "I'm ready, go ahead."

"Thank you," Kate said sincerely. "Joking aside, I cannot thank you enough."

Selina held up her palm before Kate said anything else. She quickly stood up and held out her hand. "Thank you for all your hard work, and very best wishes for the future."

Kate shook it. "I hope I'll see you again," she said.

Selina politely smiled, not prepared to say anything else. She didn't know if she would see Kate again, and she wasn't about to start mourning the possibility of this being the last time they spoke. Not only was she too busy for theatrics, she also didn't want Kate to see her reaction.

Kate inclined her head. "Goodbye, Selina."

"Goodbye, Kate."

She watched her leave, trying to ignore the heavy stone that had lodged itself in her throat.

She sat down heavily. The thank you that would have seemed like such a victory some months ago now seemed so hollow and meaningless.

Kate had been right; Selina had desperately wanted gratitude in return for her kindness. It had been her main motivation at first. Things had changed, though Selina didn't quite understand why. Or at least she wasn't ready to acknowledge why.

Her phone rang, pulling her back to reality with a shrill tone. She tore her eyes away from Kate's retreating form, silently wishing her the best as she did.

20

New Beginnings

CARRIE GESTURED TO THE NUMBER ON THE DOOR. "Home, sweet home!"

The set of keys shook in Kate's hand. She couldn't believe she was about to open the door of her own apartment. It had only been a few days before when Carrie had called her and advised that she'd pulled a few strings and had managed to get her accommodation. She'd rushed over to the council offices on her lunch hour to meet with Carrie and work her way through the necessary paperwork.

Now, she held the keys in her trembling hand.

"It's a lovely hallway," Carrie joked. "Maybe we should have a look inside now?"

Kate chuckled. "This all feels so surreal. I've been waiting for this for so long, and now it's here, I don't quite believe it."

"That's the problem with dreams coming true. We're too busy assuming the worst to actually enjoy them."

Kate took a deep breath, put the key in the lock, and

opened the door. She took a hesitant step inside and looked around. Never before had an empty, poorly decorated room ever looked so beautiful to her. The peeling paint and the scuffed doorframe just added to the charm and gave her a project to work on.

She walked into the kitchen and marvelled at a sink, a cooker, and even a microwave to call her own. These were all things she'd taken for granted in her previous homes, but not anymore. Now she would be truly grateful for everything she had.

Further exploration revealed a small living room, a bedroom, and a bathroom. Everything she needed. More than she needed.

She began to realise her cheeks were aching with a wide grin that she couldn't control.

"Happy?" Carrie asked, smiling in return.

"Ecstatic," Kate breathed. "But promise me no one is missing out because I have this place. There are so many people who have a greater need than me."

"Kate, you are a high-risk person," Carrie said firmly. "A single woman who only has a home in the evening—only if a small shelter continues to find funding to remain open *and* happens to have room for you. Your social worker should have placed you months ago."

Kate felt her cheeks heat in a blush. "I might have not pushed as hard as I could have. I was okay on the streets. I mean, it wasn't fun or anything. But when you see how some other people are living—"

"You've been lucky so far. If that shelter closed permanently, and they sometimes do, what would you have done?"

The thought had crossed Kate's mind in the past. The shelter was a lifeline. A very unstable one.

"I've worked with homeless charities," Carrie explained. "You're a typical case of someone who ended up homeless and lost their self-esteem. You look around and think that everyone else's needs come above yours. But that isn't the case, Kate. You're important, and you earned this. All I did was rattle some cages and get you what you should have been given a long time ago."

Kate knew she'd not been pushy with the council during her weekly meetings. She remembered sitting there and accepting everything they'd said about housing short-ages and people in greater need. Eventually, it had become the norm. Kate didn't ever expect to get a home from them.

Carrie was as ruthlessly efficient as Selina but kind and warm with it. Kate had instantly taken a liking to her, which had been hard, as everything in her was telling her that she'd befriended Selina's mortal enemy. She had to remind herself that Selina had encouraged this business agreement.

Carrie Lane was now her boss and fast becoming a good friend. Selina was fading into her past, whether she liked it or not.

"You're right," Kate agreed.

She looked around the room. Her bedroom. She started to think of all the things she needed to do in order to get the place habitable. Luckily, she'd earned two days' paid holiday during her time at Addington's and was tech-nically on annual leave. The money in her savings account would just be able to cover the essentials as well as bills and food for the next month until her new, and much higher, pay came through.

"Can I help you with anything else?" Carrie asked. "I don't have a meeting for another two hours, so if you need anything?"

Kate shook her head. "No, you've already done so much. Thank you. I'll be okay. I think I'll probably just spend the next hour walking around the apartment in a daze anyway."

Carrie chuckled. "Very well, I'll see you in two days. If you need anything in the meantime, you have my number." She stepped forward and wrapped Kate in a hug.

Kate returned the hug, grateful for the contact and the new boss and friend she had acquired. Carrie was very maternal in her mannerisms; Kate had noticed this in the way she interacted with staff at the charity when she went for her interview. It was going to be a very different environment to working with Ivor, something which she was looking forward to.

"Rightio, I'm off. Let me know if you need anything," Carrie said. "I'll see myself out!"

Kate said goodbye, and a few seconds later she heard the front door close.

She slowly walked from room to room, taking everything in. Tiny cracks in the wall, the new carpet in the hallway, the bathroom which had recently been scrubbed spotless, and the window in the sitting room which needed a little TLC.

The apartment had quirks that she already loved.

She sat on the floor and leaned back against the wall. It felt good to sit on soft, warm ground. To not feel the wind whipping her hair against her face. To be protected from the elements.

All the things she had once taken for granted and then lost were now back in her life. She vowed to not be so careless in ignoring them in the future. A roof over her head was a luxury she hadn't understood before.

She smiled and let out a small chuckle.

All of this had started by her rejecting Selina's offer of a free cup of coffee. If she'd accepted that drink, what would have happened? Would Selina have been so determined to force gratitude of some kind from Kate? Would she now be working for Selina's ex-wife? Probably not. If she'd taken that drink and said nothing more, she would have probably never embarked on the journey that followed.

The smile left her face as she thought about saying goodbye to Selina. It had been a hard goodbye, harder than all the rest at Addington's. This was probably because she expected more from Selina, but Kate always knew in her heart that she'd only ever receive a professional handshake and the usual speech.

Kate wanted to believe that she was more to Selina than just another member of the post room. They'd talked, shared jokes, and Kate had continued to give Selina advice on how to deal with awkward people. Advice which usually consisted of Kate suggesting that Selina be a little nicer. Advice which Selina took on board and later begrudgingly agreed had helped.

Selina was impossible to read. Kate thought they had some kind of a connection. They were not quite friends, not really work colleagues, but... something. After all,

Selina had spent a night looking for her after Abigail had kicked her out. Kate had stayed in her guestroom. And Selina had gotten her the job in the post room, ensuring she was in employment, nearby, under the watchful eye of an adorable grandfather figure.

All things Selina didn't have to do, but did.

Selina wasn't what most people would consider kind and generous. She was harsh and pragmatic. And yet, she went out of her way to help Kate.

It had been less than a day, and Kate already found herself missing Selina. Which was odd because there had been plenty of weeks at Addington's where Kate didn't see Selina for days on end.

This was different. She was no longer in the same building, just a few floors away.

"This isn't getting you anywhere," Kate told herself.

She stood up and stretched. The mystery of Selina would have to wait, possibly to never be solved.

At that moment, Kate needed to go shopping and get her new apartment in order.

21

The Final Straw

KATE WIPED AWAY THE PREVIOUS WEEK'S FIGURES from the whiteboard. She pulled the cap off the whiteboard pen with her teeth and wrote in the new date. Behind her she could hear the sound of her team taking phone calls. If she focused for long enough, she could pick out individual conversations, accents, vocal patterns, things she'd gotten to know since starting work at Parbrook Age Support three weeks before.

As a senior operator, she'd been given a lot of responsibility and in return had a voice to help shape the direction of the company.

One of the first things she had implemented was the whiteboard.

Every week she updated vital stats with call numbers, answer rates, and a satisfaction score. She wanted the team to know where they were and how they were performing. She remembered that when she first started at her old call centre, it had been helpful to see that her role was part of a bigger picture. To understand that when they worked together, they could achieve great things.

Carrie entered the office, laden down with folders and bags as usual.

"How did it go?" Kate asked.

"Great, we've secured the extra funding, so the next step is to start thinking about more staff," Carrie said. She paused by Kate and looked around the office. "We'll need more desks."

"We have the extra phone lines already," Kate explained. "I got those ordered when David was here last week. And we can rent more headsets, so that shouldn't be too expensive."

"You're an angel," Carrie said. "Drop me an email with numbers, and we can have a chat in our meeting tomorrow. Right now, I think I'm late."

Kate looked towards the boardroom where three people from another charity had been waiting a few minutes for Carrie's arrival. Luckily, most people who knew Carrie knew that she was never, ever on time.

"We got them tea and coffee. They said they didn't mind waiting," Kate said.

"Wonderful, I don't know what I'd do without you." Carrie tapped her arm as she brushed past her and into the boardroom.

"No problem," Kate called out. She turned her attention back to the piece of paper in her hand and started adding numbers from the sheet to the whiteboard.

As she looked at the date, her mind started to drift. She pictured where she was a month before, and then a month before that, and then another month in the past.

Things had changed rapidly for her over the last couple of years.

If anyone had ever told her about the train of events that would lead her to where she was, she'd never have believed them. Would have been terrified to even consider it.

She finally felt settled again. She had a job she adored, and the people she worked with were fast becoming friends. Her small apartment was starting to take shape, and she had big plans to make it into a cosy home.

She jumped at the sound of the door swinging open. It cracked loudly against the wall. Kate recalled the last time a door had cracked so loudly. She pictured Abigail's furious and tear-stained face. Her heart beat fast and she spun around.

Selina stood in the doorway, eyes darting around the room in fury. "Where is she?" she demanded.

Kate put her paperwork and pen on her desk and approached Selina. Members of the team were looking up, still taking calls but watching what was happening. They were probably wondering if they needed to take action regarding the mad woman who had just stormed into their office.

"She's in a meeting," Kate explained.

She hadn't seen Selina since she'd said goodbye to her in her office. This was hardly how she'd pictured their reunion.

"I want to see her, immediately," Selina said. She attempted to walk around Kate.

Kate sidestepped and blocked her path. "You can't. It's

an important meeting. You should call her." Her anger was rising. Selina couldn't even be bothered to say hello to her.

Selina waved a sheet of paper in Kate's face. Kate didn't have a chance to read the contents, but she didn't need to. She knew already. Carrie had been honest about how the divorce was progressing, or not progressing as the case was.

"I have been summoned to *court,*" Selina rasped.

"I'm aware. You couldn't ignore Carrie forever. She was obviously going to have to do something," Kate said. She'd lowered her voice and hoped Selina would do the same.

"I've been far too busy to deal with this ridiculous matter! And now this?"

Kate sighed. "I think you've been ignoring it. As you have been since before I met you."

"How dare you," Selina hissed. "This is nothing to do with you."

"No, how dare you!" Kate stepped into her personal space. "You could have found time, but you're so damned obsessed with getting to the thirteenth floor that you push everything else to the side. I have news for you, Selina. You're not too busy. You're just pig-headed."

"You don't know me," Selina argued. "As if you have a clue what I'm going through."

"No, I don't. I wish I did, but you're so focused on one goal that you don't see when people around you want to have a simple conversation with you. You just want that promotion so you can hang out with the other board members and screw everyone else. Never mind the little people, right? But in the meantime, you're burning every bridge you've ever created, and now you're alone and miserable."

"This is absolute rubbish," Selina scoffed.

Kate noted that she hadn't replied in her usual manner. There was no acerbic comeback, no witty comment. Selina seemed off-kilter, and Kate knew why. She was right.

"I have plenty of people in my life. Plenty!" Selina argued.

"No, you don't. Your sister doesn't know what to do with you. She tries, but you make it such hard work that it won't be long before she gives up. Your ex has to file a court motion just to get you to grant her freedom. Oh, I'm sorry, I forgot. You have a cat. But that's it."

Selina's eyes flashed with anger and… sadness?

Kate almost felt guilty.

Almost. She was too angry for the real thing.

Her back-and-forth relationship with Selina was such a mystery that she didn't know where she stood. There had been times when she'd really believed that she had something with the older woman, some kind of friendship, but then Selina had quickly put that thought to rest with her behaviour. Selina, who never even checked in to see how she was. Selina, who wanted nothing but gratitude for her own good deeds when they first met. Selina, whom she just couldn't fathom. Selina, who pushed all her buttons and more.

"So, you're an expert on me now? I take it Carrie had poisoned your mind against me." Selina folded her arms defensively across her chest.

Kate laughed bitterly. "Actually, no. Carrie hasn't said anything nasty about you at all. The only time she talks about you, she's actually quite complimentary. I'm saying this because I know you. Because I'm the person who had to tell you to pretend to give a damn about people in order for them to not treat you like dirt. The basic principle of any relationship: be a nice person. Or at least *pretend* to be one."

There was no guessing the look in Selina's eyes. Hurt. This time Kate did feel guilty; she'd gone too far.

"I can see there's nothing else to be said here," Selina said. She straightened and stared at Kate for a moment before she spun around and left as quickly as she'd arrived.

Kate took a second to catch her breath. She'd been so furious that her heart had been thudding against her ribcage and her breath had been coming in short pants.

She had no idea where the eruption of anger had come from. She wanted to run after Selina and apologise but she knew the damage had been done.

"Dammit, Kate," she muttered to herself.

22

Probation Over

It was the end of the day on her thirtieth day of employment at Parbrook Age Support. Kate thought it had been going well, but that didn't stop her from being nervous. She was due to have a meeting with Carrie to discuss whether she had passed her probationary period, and she was full of dread.

Her knee had been bouncing uncontrollably for the last two hours, and she'd skipped lunch altogether as her stomach roiled.

She cast her mind back to every little thing that had gone wrong since she started. Somehow, she couldn't think of a single improvement she'd made, even though she knew there were many. Her mind was a complete blank; all she could think of were negatives.

What was supposed to be a casual glance at an online jobs board had turned into creating an account and favouriting a few positions she thought she might be able to do.

Just in case.

"Kate?"

She looked up. Carrie was leaning around her office door. She looked apologetic.

It was then that Kate realised it was six o'clock, half an hour after the office had technically closed. She was the only person still in the call centre.

"Sorry, the call went on and on," Carrie apologised. "Are you ready?"

Kate nodded and dragged herself out of her seat. She hadn't remembered saying goodbye to anyone; she hoped she'd done it on autopilot. Most of the day was a blur. As the time of her meeting had grown closer and closer, her nerves had taken over.

"Sit down." Carrie gestured to the spare chair in the cramped office.

Carrie's office was the only private area, outside of the kitchen and the boardroom, in the company. It was a small space, with just enough room for a couple of filing cabinets, a desk, and two chairs. As usual, it was full of clutter and paperwork. Carrie was efficient, but she wasn't tidy.

"So, how do you think this last month has gone?" she asked.

Kate wanted to laugh. She had no idea. Yesterday she would have said that everything was looking great. Today, her self-confidence had taken a long-term vacation and had turned off its phone.

"Good?" Kate half-asked.

Carrie chuckled. "Are you asking me or telling me?"

"I'm not sure. How do you think it's gone?" Kate

leaned forward and rubbed her hands together, trying to get some circulation back into them.

Carrie frowned. She tilted her head and regarded Kate for a second. "I'm not sacking you, Kate."

Kate let out a breath. She felt like she had been holding it in for the last eight hours. "Really?"

"Of course I'm not," Carrie said. "You're the best employee I have. Hell, you're making me feel redundant with some of the improvements you made. Have you been worried about this?"

"All day," Kate admitted.

"Oh, sweetheart! This is just a formality. We have to have a meeting to check I'm happy with your work but also to check you're still happy working here. It's a two-way street."

Kate brought her feet up to the chair and hugged her legs. She lowered her head to her knees and took a couple of deep breaths. She'd convinced herself that something would happen and she'd be forced to leave, that Parbrook Age Support would be another organisation to add to the list of jobs she'd raced through recently.

"So," Carrie continued, "if you're happy to stay, then I'm more than happy to sign off this paperwork and consider you a permanent member of the team."

Kate lowered her legs and sat properly. She quickly nodded. "I'd really like that. Sorry about all this." She gestured to her face, which she knew was flushed. "I've been in a bit of a panic about this."

"I can tell, I'm so sorry... I didn't know you were worrying about this. If I'd known, I would have done this first thing in the morning. I only left it so we could go out for a nice meal somewhere to celebrate. If you're up to it?"

Her stomach rumbled. The panic had lifted, and hunger had quickly struck. She rubbed her hands over her face. "Yeah, give me a couple of minutes to look like a human being again."

Carrie walked around the desk and put her hand on Kate's shoulder. "I know it will take a while, but you have to start building your confidence. You deserve this job. You're damned good at it, and you must badger me for a raise in twelve months."

Kate laughed. "I'll do my best."

"Good. Now, get ready to go, and we'll head out to dinner." Carrie patted Kate's shoulder a couple more times before leaving the room.

Kate took a few deep breaths to try to centre herself. It surprised her how some days she could feel fine and then suddenly her entire world view could shift. She supposed having the rug pulled out from under you and losing everything could do that to a person.

"Get yourself together," she told herself.

And maybe speak to someone, she thought. *Or at least get a book on the subject.*

But that was a decision for another day. Right now, she had a celebratory dinner to get ready for.

Her job was safe. She smiled at the thought. Things were going to be okay.

23

Dinner Truths

"Refill?" Carrie held the bottle of white wine up.

Kate considered it for a moment. The last thing she wanted was to turn up for work the next day with a hangover. She'd not eaten a lot that day, but the bread basket and the filling pasta meal had sucked up most of the alcohol from the first two glasses of wine.

And she was celebrating. She nodded and pushed her glass towards Carrie. "Thank you."

Carrie poured liquid into Kate's glass and then her own. "No, thank *you*. It's nice to have someone to share a bottle of wine with."

"I thought you were seeing someone?" Kate asked.

"I am, but she doesn't drink." Carrie put the bottle back into the ice bucket. "I try to be supportive, so I don't drink at home very often. But when I go out to a nice restaurant, a glass of wine feels essential."

"I've never really drunk much," Kate said. "It's never really been something I enjoyed. My ex drank like a fish, and my parents did, too. That's probably what turned me off of it."

Carrie nodded her understanding.

It had been a lovely meal, and they were now waiting to see if their stomachs would allow a tiny wedge of space for dessert. They'd talked about work for a while but had quickly changed to more personal topics. Kate felt like she could be honest with Carrie. She was the maternal figure that Kate had always wanted but never had.

The wine had taken the edge off her nerves, and a question that she'd been dying to ask was floating to the front of her mind. It was something she'd wanted to know for ages but that seemed a little too personal. No worries, though, the third glass of wine was taking care of any scruples.

"Can I ask you a question?" Kate blurted out.

Carrie didn't hesitate. "Sure!"

"What happened with you and Selina?"

It was out there. Kate wondered if Carrie would answer or if she had gone a step too far.

Carrie sipped her wine and gently placed her glass back on the table. "We fell in love very quickly, got married even faster. We didn't think it through at all. It was a recipe for disaster."

"How so?"

Carrie played with her wine glass. "Selina is very strong-willed. She's a go-getting, no-nonsense kind of person. I'm more of a go-with-the-flow individual. While those things may sometimes go together, in my experience, it doesn't work out. I'm as much to blame as she is.

"I caved in to everything she suggested, even if I knew

it was a bad idea. Selina is so confident and powerful that it's easy to go along with whatever she says. Even if it seemed to be the most terrible idea in the world, I'd find myself thinking that she must know what she's doing. Her choice of decorating, holiday, car, career choices, everything. Whatever she said, I'd agree because I thought it was the right thing."

Kate could see that playing out. Carrie did sometimes struggle to make decisions and was always asking for confirmation and advice from the team. Kate had initially thought it was her management style, but soon realised that Carrie was someone who didn't like confrontation.

"I think Selina hated that I never stood up for myself," she said. "And I think she resented that I let her do whatever she wanted, even if I thought it was a bad idea. Because, when things invariably went wrong, I would tell her that I never thought it was a good idea in the first place. Which would obviously frustrate her. And so, we argued. A lot."

"Sounds rough," Kate admitted.

"It was pretty awful. We were just not the right people to be together. I loved Selina. In fact, I still do in many ways. I just know that we're not right for each other at all. She's a good person under all her hard-ass bravado."

"Yeah, I kinda thought there was a good heart under all the ice," Kate agreed. "She pretty much saved my life. But then, I don't know. She's hard to read. One minute I think she's a good person, the next I doubt myself."

"She's a tough nut," Carrie agreed.

"When I first saw her, I was spending my days in a sleeping bag in the car park behind her office."

Carrie smiled. "Oh, I bet she *loved* that."

Kate chuckled. "Yeah, I was really classing the place up. One evening she's walking across the car park, all power suit and attitude. She's on her phone, saying that her nephews were snivelling little runts and she didn't ask to be an aunt, so why should she bother to know their names or put time aside to see them. She seemed like a really nasty piece of work."

Carrie wiped tears of laughter away from her cheeks. "Yup, sounds like her."

"She goes to the coffee shop, and on her way back she is still on the phone but places a takeaway mug in front of me." Kate shook her head at the memory. "And she doesn't speak to me, doesn't even *look* at me. And I'm thinking this rude woman can't even be bothered to look at me while she's complaining about how terrible her privileged life is."

"What did you do?"

"I told her I didn't want it."

Carrie burst out laughing. "No!"

"Yep. I told her I didn't want her drink. I'd seen her type before, people who don't really want to do good, just want to either be seen to be doing good, or feel like they've made a difference when really they'd rather you didn't exist. I once had a woman film herself giving me fifty pence, monologuing about how it was everyone's duty to help those less well off than them. You know, on Facebook Live probably."

Carrie nodded quickly. "Poverty porn."

Kate blinked. "Sorry?"

"No, seriously, it's a thing. Like when we send some

white megastar to Africa for a day so they can hug a black baby and tell everyone back home to donate money to a cause. It's changed a bit now that anyone with a phone and an Internet connection can instantly stream to a potential audience of millions. Someone sees someone in need, but rather than silently doing a good thing, they tell everyone what they are doing and explain the horrors the person they helped had to go through. It's exploitative for entertainment."

Kate snapped her fingers. "Exactly! Yes. That's what people do. I saw another woman photographing her daughter giving me money."

"Disgraceful." Carrie shook her head in disgust.

Kate sipped some wine. "Obviously, Selina didn't do that. But I didn't know if she was giving me the drink because she wanted to help me or if she just wanted to feel better about herself. And she seemed so mean that I didn't want anything to do with her."

"So you said no."

"I was polite. I said, 'No, thank you.'" Kate chuckled.

"I bet that annoyed her."

"Yeah, she said I should learn to accept charity, considering my situation. Which was probably a fair point. Anyway, I didn't accept the drink. The next day Julian, the manager of the coffee shop, came over to me and told me they did community outreach programs and offered me an unpaid job."

Carrie smiled. "Oh, I wonder how that happened."

"I didn't put two and two together. It was only later that day, when Selina came in and introduced herself as my *guardian angel*, that I realised she'd had a part to play."

Carrie snorted a laugh.

"And then she wanted me to say thank you. Like it was weighing on her mind that she hadn't gotten a thank you the day before, that she'd had to up the ante to something I had to be grateful for." Kate shrugged. "I told her I wouldn't grovel for the rest of my life, and that was the end of it."

"And was it?" Carrie asked.

Kate looked at her wine glass as she considered the question. "Not really," she admitted. "I've always been grateful to Selina for that. I know I have a lot to thank her for, but I won't tell her that. At this point, she knows. She doesn't need me to tell her. If anything, I enjoy giving her a hard time about things."

Carrie picked up a breadstick from the bread basket and bit off the end. "I never gave Selina a hard time about anything," she said. "Which is why we ended up the way we are. She needs someone to challenge her. But I don't know if she'll find someone, as she's so afraid of getting hurt that she pushes people away to keep herself safe. It just means she ends up alone." Carrie looked at Kate. "She needs someone like you."

Kate felt her cheeks heat up instantly. She grabbed her wine and took a sip. When it had cleared her throat, she shook her head. "No, Selina would never be interested in someone like me."

Carrie dropped the breadstick, snapped her fingers, and pointed at Kate. She grinned happily. "I knew it!"

Kate sat back a little in surprise. "Knew what?"

"You like her!"

"I don't!" Kate quickly denied.

"You do. You absolutely do! Because you've just said that *Selina* wouldn't be interested in someone like *you*. Not that you're not interested in her."

Kate shook her head. "You're delusional."

"No, you're in denial. And this is your lack of self-confidence making itself known again. You are interested, aren't you? I thought so. The way you talk about her made me think you were interested, and now I'm certain."

"I can't believe I'm talking about this with you, her *ex-wife*." Kate covered her face with her hands.

"Soon to be," Carrie corrected.

Kate lowered her hands, blew out a breath, and looked at the ceiling for a second. She lowered her eyes again to Carrie. "It doesn't matter what I want. It would never work between us. We're very different people, and she'd never look twice at someone as young as me."

Carrie casually shrugged. "Selina's dated younger women."

Kate wasn't ready for this conversation. She snatched up the dessert menu. "Anyway."

Carrie took the menu out of her hand with a grin. "We're not done talking."

"We are." Kate laughed and took the menu back. "I'm thinking cheesecake."

"I'm thinking you should ask Selina on a date. I'm also thinking chocolate. Whatever has the most chocolate on that dessert menu must be mine."

With that, the subject was dropped.

But Kate couldn't stop thinking about it. Not as they tucked into dessert, and not later, as she brushed her teeth in her small bathroom. She wondered if it was the wine, but secretly knew that wasn't the case. Selina was always lurking in the recesses of her mind.

And yet, it was all irrelevant after the last encounter they had. Selina clearly wasn't interested in her, as she'd gone weeks without getting in touch, but the argument in Carrie's office was scorched into Kate's memory.

She'd said things she shouldn't have. She'd been upset that Selina didn't care about her in the way she cared about Selina. In the end, she had lashed out and said things that she knew hurt the older woman.

Her interest in Selina was completely immaterial, though, she knew as she got into bed and turned out the light. Selina would never think of her as anything more than the homeless girl she'd once helped, who had then had the audacity to shout her down in a crowded call centre.

24

Being Played

IT WAS NINE O'CLOCK IN THE EVENING. THE CLEANERS had come and gone, and the office was silent. Silent except for the sound of Selina Hale's fingers dancing across her laptop keyboard as she replied to emails.

It had been hard work, but she had managed to turn things around for Addington's. It had taken a lot of creative accountancy, cutbacks, and an encouragement that the board take over a smaller firm, which would enable them to provide new services currently missing from their portfolio.

Then there had been the landmark moment where Margaret's event had fallen woefully short of expectations. Selina gloated as she remembered how she had finally been able to cut the marketing budget to a more reasonable figure.

The digitisation project she had set in motion two years ago had completed its final phase, which meant that their storage, copying, and postage fees had dropped by more than half. The cuts and savings meant that budget could be reallocated towards strategies that she knew worked, which meant a growing portfolio of clients.

The future figures were looking good, and Selina knew the credit lay directly at her door.

It had been worth the long hours, the weekends, the emergency meetings, and the sucking up to board members. Addington's was financially secure for the foreseeable future. In fact, it was flourishing.

It was just a matter of time before Selina would be out of her current office and up on the thirteenth floor where she belonged. She was looking forward to the change, and the break from the long hours.

She'd always known that the climb to the top would be long and arduous, but the last few weeks had pushed her to her limits. Holiday brochures were stacked neatly in the bottom drawer of her filing cabinet, a reminder that she'd take a well-deserved and long overdue break before taking her place upstairs.

Her mobile phone rang, and Jonathan Addington's name appeared on the screen. It was unusual for Jonathan to call so late at night, which probably meant it was very good news.

"Good evening, Jonathan," she said smoothly.

"Selina, I hope I'm not disturbing anything?" he asked.

"No, not at all. Just finishing up some emails."

"At this hour?" He sounded shocked but pleased. "You always impress me."

"Thank you," she preened. "I try my best."

"Well, I hope you're sitting down because I have good news."

This is it, she thought, gripping the edge of the desk. *At last, everything has come together.*

"I am. What's the news?" she asked.

"I just had dinner with my father," Jonathan said.

Good, she thought. Any confirmation of a new board member would have to be approved by Nicholas Addington himself. She leaned back in her chair, unable to keep the grin from spreading across her face.

"He is *finally* standing down!" Jonathan exclaimed with far too much excitement for a man of his age and standing. "I knew it was coming, but I thought it wouldn't be for another six to twelve months."

Selina gripped the phone a little tighter. She hadn't expected that. Nicholas hadn't given any indication of his intentions to stand down. In fact, the last time succession was even mentioned he claimed he planned to stay in his role for at least another five to ten years.

Her mind tossed the statement over and over while she considered any possible course of action that might follow. She was frantically trying to figure out what had happened before Jonathan had a chance to verbalise it.

"Oh," she said. It was all her brain would give her.

Nicholas leaving means Jonathan will take his place, she thought. *Which means he'll want to fill the board with his golfing chums, and there won't be a thing his father can do about it.*

A sinking feeling surged through her.

Her plan had always been to work as hard as possible to show her worth to Nicholas Addington, a man known for rewarding hard work. She'd watched Nicholas for years and had studied him, made it her business to understand the way he worked. Because of that, she'd always known that he was the type of person who would see her efforts and give her a comfortable board position as a thank you.

Jonathan wasn't like his father at all. Jonathan didn't reward hard work, he exploited it. His mantra was that work someone else did was work he didn't have to do.

She'd made a terrible miscalculation. She had to remind herself to breathe.

"I'll be taking his place, obviously," Jonathan explained. He sounded giddy with excitement.

"Obviously," Selina said. "Congratulations."

Things were finally slotting into place in her brain. She felt sick. She'd built her whole strategy around one concrete fact, that Nicholas Addington would remain the head of the board. It had never even occurred to her that he wouldn't. That was turning out to be a massive miscalculation.

It seemed so obvious now, so very clear for her to see. Of course Nicholas would want to retire when the company was at its peak. No one wanted to leave a company which was struggling.

The economic landscape had been difficult over the last few years, and Addington's had taken its fair share of knocks. Selina had always fought to bring it back. This time she'd outdone herself; this time Addington's was stronger than it had been in years.

Which meant it was the perfect time for Nicholas to stand down and be praised by his peers for his magnificent leadership.

She had brought it all on herself.

"Thing is, I can't make too many board changes too

quickly," Jonathan was saying. "I don't want to spook the investors, especially now. We need to be perceived to be strong and stable. And you know how board changes can set tongues wagging."

"I see."

"I have some people I really need to bring on board immediately. Colin and Tim, obviously," he explained. "Once my dad leaves, I think Peter and Mike will leave soon after. They are near retirement and will probably see this as a great time to go. I'll need to plug those positions with David. Maybe Craig. There's a lot to think about. But what I wanted to say was, you are on my radar, Selina. Don't worry. I can't move quickly on this, but as soon as I am able to, that position upstairs is all yours."

She knew it was a lie. She felt light-headed, and she gripped the phone so tightly she was surprised it didn't shatter.

"I'm grateful for that, Jonathan," she said slowly, professionally.

"Great! Excellent! Well, keep up the good work, Selina. And hopefully, in twelve months or so, we'll have that chat."

"I look forward to it," she replied.

He hung up the call, and Selina lowered the phone from her ear.

She tried to remember to breathe in and out, but the room was spinning so fast she couldn't catch up.

It was all becoming clear to her.

She'd been played.

Jonathan had been the one to tell her that Nicholas wouldn't retire yet. She clearly remembered him telling her more than once that his father would be staying for another decade. But he'd just let slip that he'd known it was coming. He had expected Nicholas to leave within the year.

He'd deliberately fed Selina false information, and she'd fallen for it.

Jonathan wanted to take over. He knew his father wouldn't leave Addington's unless it was in a strong financial position. He knew Selina wanted a place on the board, and he knew she was the only one with the drive and planning to be able to pull off such a turnaround.

Now Jonathan would step in and reward his friends. The boys club. He'd keep Selina exactly where she was, because she was the only person in the company who could do what she could do. What he *needed* her to do. In other words, he had no incentive to promote her.

She'd been so focused on her goal that she hadn't stopped to consider the bigger picture. Now she couldn't believe she'd been so foolish.

She felt cold, empty. Lethargic. More than that, she felt lost. Like she suddenly had no idea where she was or where she was going.

She reached forward and closed the lid of her laptop and slowly stood up. She packed up her bag, took her coat from the rack, and walked out of her office.

She turned off the lights as she left, standing in the dark corridor while she waited for the elevator. For the first time in years, she had no idea what she was going to do. The world felt off-kilter, like she didn't know what would happen next.

She left the building in a daze and sat in the driver's

seat of her car. She didn't know how long she sat there, staring out of the windscreen at the building.

For a brief moment, she considered calling her sister until she remembered that they still weren't speaking following their argument. She'd meant to call but had never got around to it.

Too busy with work.

As usual.

Working towards a goal that would never happen. Being played by someone she'd always considered to be an idiot.

Now that idiot was celebrating a promotion while Selina was left counting the hours she'd wasted. Time she could have spent living her life had been spent working towards a promotion that would never come.

You're alone and miserable, she heard Kate's voice echo in her head.

She was right. She had burnt every bridge until she was left with no one. The only people she really talked to these days were work contacts—certainly not anyone she would consider a friend in a time of crisis.

She pictured Kate in her mind. She supposed Kate would get a kick out of hearing what had happened to her. She wondered if she should call and tell her that she'd been right in everything she'd said. That way, she could at least hear a semi-friendly voice. If Kate would even speak to her.

She unlocked her phone and scrolled down to the number of the cheap phone she had given Kate all those weeks before. As her thumb hovered over the call button, she wondered what she would say.

She stabbed the button, deciding that she'd figure it out as she went along. Right then, she just wanted to hear Kate's voice. Almost immediately she heard a strange tone and a robotic voice informed her that the number had been disconnected.

She got a new number, Selina realised. She licked her dry lips and hung up the call.

It made sense. Kate didn't need her anymore, so why would she keep the number? She'd moved on. Kate had gone up in the world while Selina had stalled at the twelfth floor.

A bitter laugh escaped her as she realised two things in quick succession. Firstly, Kate now worked in a call centre for old people who were lonely. Secondly, she was an old person who was lonely.

She wanted to speak to Kate. For some reason, that was all she could focus on.

She searched for the charity online and took a deep breath before pressing a button to connect the call. It rang a few times before she heard Kate's voice. Sadly, it was a pre-recorded message telling her that the office was closed for the night and urging her to call back in the morning.

"Your call is really important to us," Kate's voice said.

Selina hung up. She leaned her forehead on the cold glass of the driver's side window and blew out a long breath.

"What now?" she mumbled to herself.

Unexpected Behaviour

KATE DUMPED HER BAG AND COAT ON HER CHAIR AND snatched her notepad from her desk. She was late to work for the first time. She didn't think she could possibly be blamed for it as Carrie had been the one to insist that they stay out late. And Carrie had bought that *third* bottle of wine.

She hurried across the office before stopping, turning back, and snagging a pen from her desk.

"Rough night?" Jasmine, her desk neighbour, asked with a grin.

"Yeah, I think I'm still asleep," Kate admitted.

She checked she had everything and rushed to Carrie's office where she had been due to start a meeting ten minutes ago. Thankfully, it was only a meeting for the two of them. Kate would have felt mortified if she'd kept more people waiting because peeling her face from her pillow had been such hard work that morning.

She poked her head around the corner. Carrie was on the phone, a confused expression on her face. She blinked up at Kate and gestured towards the chair in front of her desk.

Kate sat silently, wondering what the call was about.

"I see. Well…" Carrie trailed off, seemingly at a loss for words.

Kate fiddled with the cap of her pen, spinning it around and around. She felt uncomfortable, even though Carrie had invited her in.

"I suppose that's that." Carrie sat back in her chair. "I mean, after the final paperwork."

Kate looked at the walls, anything to distract her.

"Of course, well, I appreciate the call. Thank you for letting me know." Carrie leaned forward and hung up the call. She stared at the desk phone for a few moments.

"Is everything okay?" Kate asked.

"Selina's signed the divorce papers," Carrie said. "Quite unexpectedly. They were hand-delivered sometime last night. All signed and completed."

"That's good news," Kate said without feeling. It was good news, but also extremely unexpected news. "Did you speak to her last night?"

"No." Carrie slowly shook her head. "Should I call her?"

Kate shrugged. "I don't know. Do you think you should?"

"I… don't know either. This seems so unlike her. Selina is like a dog with a bone. For her to just silently give up and sign the papers… it's not like her at all."

"Maybe she thought enough time had passed?" Kate suggested.

Carrie leaned back in her chair and looked thoughtfully at the ceiling. "No, that's not very likely. It's all a bit strange."

They sat in silence for a few moments before Carrie shook her head and reached for a folder of paperwork. "I'm sorry, we better get this meeting started before we run out of time."

She shuffled through papers, looking for her meeting notes. Kate could tell that she was concerned but was trying not to show it.

Even Kate knew that caving in like this was not Selina's style. If Selina was intending to deliver signed documents, she'd do it stylishly and publicly. Kate could imagine Selina strutting through the office and dramatically removing her sunglasses while pinning Carrie with a glare before slamming down the divorce papers.

That was how Selina Hale did things.

Silently posting an envelope one evening was not at all how Selina did things.

"Here we are." Carrie pulled a report from a stack of paperwork. "Now, we need to have a look at the call duration report for last month because there's an anomaly."

Kate looked through her own paperwork and pulled out a copy of the report. She'd already seen the anomaly and had a reason for it. She'd gotten to know the system and all its quirks during her month at Parbrook Age Support.

She showed Carrie the report and her findings, explaining the small bug in the system and the best ways to go about repairing it, but her mind was distracted. She knew she shouldn't be thinking about Selina, certainly not worrying about her.

But it was beyond her control.

Like the bug in the call centre software, Selina's behaviour was a mystery. And Kate didn't like unexplained loose ends. Something had caused Selina to suddenly change her mind about the divorce, and she knew she wouldn't rest until she knew what it was.

It had been a while since she'd seen any of her old colleagues at Addington's, and she wondered if it wouldn't be a good time to swing by her former workplace and say hello to a few people.

While she was there, she could see Selina for herself. Just to put her mind at ease.

26

Checking In

"My, my!" Ivor stood up and walked towards Kate, an enormous grin on his face. "Hello, stranger."

"Hello, boss," Kate greeted. She bent down a little and gave the man a hug.

"Were we expecting you?" he asked. He threaded his thumbs into the belt loops of his trousers, a pose which Kate was sad to say she missed. She knew she'd never forget a thing about her time in the basement of the accountancy firm. It had been an interesting place to work. It felt safe and like she was part of a work family who truly cared for her. On the other hand, she'd never seen such bizarre work practices. She hoped they'd never change.

"No, just passing the building and thought I'd pop in," she lied.

In truth, she'd hurried to get her work out of the way so she could rush across town and see as many people as possible before they left for the day. She was in no hurry to get to Selina's office, knowing that the woman rarely left the office before seven.

Also, she wanted to ensure she ticked everyone else off her list first. That way she would be able to finish her visit with Selina and take up as much time as she was offered.

"It's very good to see you. Are you enjoying your new job? If not…" Ivor turned and pointed towards a beaten-up old office chair which had unofficially become Kate's during her tenure in the basement. "We'd love to have you back."

"I'd love to come back, but I really like my new job," Kate admitted.

The smile never left Ivor's face, even as he nodded.

Kate suspected that Ivor's sweet nature covered a very insightful personality. He didn't talk much about himself. Vague comments about a career in the army and the occasional mention of a loving family were few and far between.

Ivor was a listener. He often sat quietly while the staff spoke loudly over the general noise of the post room. Kate noticed, even if the others didn't. She'd noticed that the older man was a fatherly figure to many, and that Ivor took that responsibility very seriously. He never gossiped but seemed to know about everything. He'd given her many a knowing look during her short time working for him.

He patted her arm. "Well, if anything changes, then we would love to have you back with us."

The post room had been boring and labour-intensive, definitely not a job Kate would willingly return to, but the knowledge that it was there in an emergency was a relief. It was nice to have a plan B for a change.

In one of her recurring nightmares, she was suddenly homeless again. Everything went wrong, and she was back to being a nobody with nothing to her name.

That seemed unlikely now. She had friends, a roof over her head, and a job she loved and was seemingly good at. The road to homelessness, from her current circumstances, seemed like a long one, but Kate had experienced it once before and knew that anything was possible.

Part of the healing process was accepting that she now had a support network who would prevent that from happening. Trusting and leaning on that support network was a step on the road to her emotional recovery.

"Thank you, Ivor, I'll definitely let you know."

Ivor turned and looked around the empty room. "I'm afraid everyone else has already left. Early to rise, and all that."

"It's okay, I just wanted to say hello to you," Kate confessed. "I'll come back another time and say hello to everyone else."

"You be sure that you do." His smile was infectious, and Kate felt that he was truly happy for her to be in better circumstances than when they'd first met.

She jutted her thumb towards the ceiling. "Better go and say hello to a few other people. Take care, Ivor."

"You too, my dear," he said.

———

Kate had seen everyone she wanted to except the person she'd actually come to check up on. The elevator doors finally opened at the twelfth floor. She stepped out and took a deep, calming breath.

She never knew what to expect from Selina. A half smile, a cold stare, a shouting match, an olive branch. And yet, despite the confusion, she still found herself eager to see the woman.

The first thing she noticed, though, was that Selina's office was empty and the lights were off. Her heart sank. Had she somehow managed to pick the only day the woman went home early?

"Hi, can I help you?"

Kate looked at what she thought of as Gemma's desk. Someone else sat there now, someone who looked confused, harassed, and exhausted. All the symptoms of working for Selina.

"I'm looking for Selina," Kate said and pointed towards the office.

The woman laughed. "You and everyone else!" She turned back to her computer and continued typing.

"I'm sorry, who are you?" Kate asked.

"Alison, Selina's PA. But, no, I don't know where she is. No, she's not contacted me," Alison said with a tone of utter exhaustion.

"I'm Kate." She held out her hand, eager to befriend Alison and find out what was happening.

Alison shook her hand and looked apologetic. "Sorry, it's been a hell of a day."

"I bet," Kate said sympathetically. "She didn't turn up this morning?"

"Nope. And no word from her. She's missed a ton of meetings. Won't reply to emails or phone calls, even to her home number." Alison shook her head and returned to her computer. "And now *my* inbox is exploding. Like I'm her keeper or something."

Kate felt the edges of panic start to wrap around her. It seemed beyond strange that Selina would vanish, and certainly not without contacting anyone.

"So, no one knows where she is?" Kate asked.

Alison looked at Kate thoughtfully for a moment. She stood up and peeked around the office to check if they were alone. "There's a rumour," she whispered, plopping herself back in her chair and leaning forward.

"Oh, yes?" Kate asked, leaning in.

"Nicholas Addington is out," Alison said, "and apparently his son Jonathan is in charge. Which means a board shake-up. So, maybe Selina is finally going to get to the thirteenth floor?"

Kate frowned. "Seems weird that she'd vanish after hearing that," she said.

Alison nodded. "True. But the rumour is that there are going to be a lot of big changes around here soon." She shrugged. "Maybe she was fired?"

Even Kate knew that Addington's needed Selina. Yes, there were a lot of very competent people in the company, but Selina was the person who steered them all. She was more than just the operations director, and everyone knew it.

"Did she have any meetings with any board members today?" Kate asked.

Alison nodded. "She was due to meet with Angus."

"Did Angus cancel?"

"No, I had to let his secretary know that Selina wasn't here."

"And the meeting was still in his diary?" Kate pressed.

"I think so, why?" Alison asked.

"He would have known if she'd been fired. He wouldn't have expected her to attend the meeting if she was," Kate explained.

How does this woman work for Selina? Kate asked herself. She couldn't follow a simple thread and make an easy assumption. In fact, the only reason she seemed to care at all about Selina's disappearance was because it was causing her extra work. It was impressive that Selina hadn't torn her to pieces yet.

"Oh, yeah." Alison looked blank for a moment. "Oh, well." She shrugged again and turned her attention back to her computer.

Kate glanced at the empty office once more. She felt bad for Selina that no one seemed to be worried about her. If anything, her absence was considered inconvenient. She couldn't entirely blame them. Selina hadn't exactly gone out of her way to be friendly to anyone. Why would they care that she vanished? Kate imagined that some people were ecstatic at the prospect of a Selina-free day.

She walked back towards the elevator and wondered what Nicholas leaving had meant for Selina. Was it promotion? Was it disappointment?

Selina's whole life seemed to centre on getting to the thirteenth floor of the building, so Kate couldn't imagine what effect that being snatched away from her would have. But if she'd been promoted, then where was she?

She entered the elevator and selected the ground floor. She reached into her bag and pulled out her mobile phone. She unlocked the device and toyed with the idea of calling Selina.

She bit her lip as she wondered what she would say, and if it was even her place to call. Turning up at the office pretending to have been passing by was one thing, actively calling Selina was entirely another.

Fragments of their argument flashed in her mind, and she wondered if Selina would even want to talk to her. She dropped her phone back into her bag.

"Everything is fine," she muttered to herself. "She's fine. And even if she wasn't, she doesn't need you."

She stepped out of the elevator, crossed the lobby, and waved goodbye to the security guards. She started to walk home, crossing the road, and looking towards the car park where she had first met Selina and started the rollercoaster journey of the last few months.

Remaining homeless could have been disastrous for her. She'd known so many people who hadn't been as lucky as she had. People who'd died from malnutrition, cold, injury, or worse.

Selina had saved her from that life. Not that Kate placed her entire salvation at the feet of the older woman. No, she was realistic about these things. Kate knew that her own motivation, determination, and hard work had helped her to achieve the things she had, but Selina had been the one to take that first chance on her. Even if it had been for selfish reasons. The fact remained that, without Selina's actions, Kate wouldn't be where she was today.

She groaned and paused walking.

She couldn't leave things the way they were. She had to know Selina was okay. Even if that meant the older woman shouted at her for getting in touch.

She opened her bag again and picked up her phone.

27

Flirting?

Selina couldn't understand why she had never quit her job before. Walking out was hugely enjoyable. Not that she could quite remember walking out. She assumed she had done so, she'd meant to at any rate. Everything was quite hazy, and she was having trouble recalling what had happened and when.

"I'm not sure you should have any more."

Selina looked at the bartender and pouted. She knew she was pouting, assumed she looked ridiculous, and yet she did it anyway.

"You've been here for hours. You're completely wasted," the bartender pushed.

"But I'm having fun," Selina replied. She turned on her stool and gestured to the pub. Behind her was a scattering of people. "With my new friends."

She'd not spoken to a single one of them. As far as she was aware. She cocked her head to one side and tried to piece together a timeline from her arrival at the pub to her current drink order. It was hard work, and she quickly gave up.

The bartender smiled kindly. "Lady, you've sat on that stool for the last four hours, ordered far too many drinks, and muttered to yourself the whole time."

Selina pushed her empty glass forward another inch. "I'm working up my courage. I'm shy…" She looked at the bartender's name badge. She squinted and stared at the young woman's chest for quite some time as she waited for the letters stopped jumping around. "…Yvonne," she finished lamely.

"One more drink," Yvonne said. "Then you should probably go home. Can I at least get you some food with that?"

Selina felt her stomach roll at the very thought of food. She shook her head and waved her credit card towards Yvonne. "I'm not hungry."

Yvonne cleared the empty glass away and turned to prepare Selina a fresh drink.

Selina leaned her head on her hand and let out a long sigh. She knew she was drunk. She was intoxicated, not idiotic. It was by design. At some point the previous night she had decided that being sober was entirely overrated. Suddenly she understood the desire of some to drink their problems away.

She'd gone from one place to another, briefly stopping at home to raid her own wine cabinet, while boring Parbrook decided to sleep, before heading out again. Her brow furrowed, a memory of signing some documents floated just out of reach.

The more she thought about it, the harder it was to grasp the thought.

She shook her head. It didn't matter now. Nothing mattered now. She'd been screwed over, and now she intended to remain drunk until she came up with a plan. A plan for what the hell she was going to do with her life.

Yvonne placed a drink in front of her and held the payment machine out. Selina held her credit card up and chased the machine around, finally capturing it and hearing the beep that indicated the payment had been successful.

"Gotcha," she muttered.

"Seriously, lady, think about going home soon." Yvonne handed her a receipt and then left to serve someone at the other end of the bar.

Selina ignored her. She had no desire to go home. And no desire to go to work. It was a weird feeling to no longer want to go to work, something that had been such an integral part of her life for so long.

Admittedly, it was nice to no longer feel like she was in a constant battle with time. No more rushing to her next meeting. No more next meeting. In fact, she didn't even know what time it was.

"Hey." Someone sat on the stool next to her. Selina turned and saw a woman looking at her. She was in her thirties, had long, blonde hair, and was casually dressed in jeans and a smart, white, plunge-neck top.

"Hello," Selina greeted. She squinted a little at the woman, wondering if she knew her. Things had gotten more and more hazy recently.

"I'm Meghan."

Selina shook her outstretched hand. The grip was firm, and her smile was wide. "Selina."

"Nice to meet you, Selina, and nice pin." Meghan pointed to something on Selina's chair.

She turned and glanced behind her. Her jacket was slung over the back of the stool, the rainbow pin that she always wore clearly visible.

"Thank you," she said. The world spun a little bit when she sat up again.

"I'd buy you a drink, but it looks like someone got there before me." Meghan indicated Selina's full glass with a nod of her head. She leaned forward and placed her hand softly on Selina's knee. "My friend got sick of me staring at you from afar and told me to come over and introduce myself."

"Oh." Selina was pretty sure this Meghan person was flirting. It had been so long that she wasn't really sure what constituted flirting any more.

Meghan sat up, her warm hand leaving Selina's knee. She raised her hand and gestured for Yvonne's attention.

Selina felt someone approach her on the other side. She turned her head to see another tall, elegant woman. She smiled as she pulled up a stool and dragged it close to Selina.

"I'm Rach."

"Hello," Selina greeted.

"So, Selina," Meghan said, "I don't see a ring. Please don't break my heart and tell me that you're married?"

Definitely flirting, Selina's brain confirmed.

"Divorced," Selina replied. A memory tried to

valiantly fight its way to the surface, but was quickly over-powered by the booze.

"Her loss," Rach said. "I'm assuming her?"

Selina nodded.

"Told you," Rach spoke over Selina's head to Meghan. "And you were afraid to come over here. I have better gaydar than you do."

"She does," Meghan replied.

Selina felt a little dizzy from whipping her head from one side to the other to keep up with the conversation. The two women kept talking, and Selina did her best to keep up. More drinks appeared at the bar, and some sort of drinking game ensued.

With one of the women on each side of her, Selina didn't want to be rude. Besides, it was good to take her mind off events. She felt a hand on her back. Meghan's hand. And it didn't feel at all innocent.

It was nice to be wanted. Even if she felt like her head was spinning.

A small glass was placed in her hand. A shot. And judging by the empty shot glasses on the bar in front of her, it wasn't her first. She hesitated for a moment, realising that she was beyond drunk. She was struggling to remember anything.

"Wait." Selina lowered her glass.

She needed a second to clear her mind a little. She was quickly becoming lost.

"I need a minute," she said.

Without warning, warm lips pressed against hers. It had been a long time since Selina had received any phys-ical affection. She quickly gave way and allowed Meghan to kiss her fully, kissing Meghan in turn. It was messy, which was probably her own fault.

She felt bereft when it ended suddenly.

"Come home with me," was whispered in her ear. "Please."

She couldn't remember replying. More discussion went over her head. Another drink was pressed into her hand. They told her that they were housemates, they lived nearby. She felt hesitant. Something told her it was wrong. She pushed that thought to one side. It had been forever since she'd let herself go and had some fun. She couldn't recall ever having a one-night stand.

The next thing she knew, she was walking towards the door, one of the women on each elbow. Something felt off, probably because she was drunk and seemed to be losing snippets of time. The last hour was merely a series of snapshots in her mind. She wondered if she was blacking out or simply forgetting events.

She'd never been truly drunk, she had no frame of reference for what it felt like. Even if she did, she knew she was too far gone to be able to recall it anyway.

A feeling pushed its way to the surface. Something important.

"My bag," she muttered as she touched her shoulders to locate it.

"Shh." Meghan hushed her and kissed her again.

Selina found herself being pressed against a wall. An outside wall. The cold air whipped around them, and she felt her sleeve being pulled up. A hand wrapping itself around her wrist. Meghan kissed her as if she were a lifeline. Selina clung to her uselessly, only the wall was keeping her upright now.

In the distance she heard shouting. Lips were torn from hers, and she started to stumble to the floor. The sound of footsteps hitting the cobbled street was deafening, so she winced and covered her ears. The noise was getting to be too much as shouts and footsteps merged into one loud din. Selina just wanted it out of her head.

Then she felt soft hands holding her face. These weren't demanding and impatient like before. These felt warm and calming.

She opened her eyes and waited for the blur of colours to stop spinning.

"Selina?"

She frowned, wincing at the pain from the simple gesture.

"Are you okay?"

Her vision cleared slowly, and she realised she was face to face with Kate.

28

Come Home

KATE LOOKED INTO SELINA'S EYES, WONDERING WHAT on earth had happened to her. Selina was always so cool, calm, and collected. Now she was sprawled out on the ground and looked to be drunk, maybe even drugged. Her eyes were wild and unfocused, and she looked lost and dazed.

"Can you sit up?" Kate asked.

Selina's eyes darted around, trying to take in the situation but seemingly not able to.

Kate took Selina by her forearms and gently sat her upright. Selina's long legs didn't cooperate, and Kate realised she had little control over her body by that point. Kate couldn't ever remember being so drunk that she flailed about in the street. From what she knew about Selina, this was most definitely not the norm for her either. Kate tugged Selina's skirt down to cover her as much as possible. She straightened her top in an attempt to make her look a little more presentable. A little more like herself.

"How are you here?" Selina slurred.

"How did I know you were here?" Kate clarified.

Selina nodded through a wince, her hand raising to her head.

"I called you, remember?"

Selina looked thoughtful but then shook her head.

"I called and asked how you were. You sounded drunk, and I asked where you were. You told me you were here, and I said to stay put because I was coming to get you."

Selina looked confused.

"Do you remember any of that?" Kate asked.

"No," Selina whispered. She looked around in confusion, and Kate's heart clenched for her. She looked so lost. This was not the adorable drunken Selina that Carrie had implied. That worried Kate because it meant that Selina was operating completely outside her normal personality.

"She took my bag," Selina said.

"Yeah, they mugged you, I tried to go after them, but I…" Kate trailed off. Adrenaline was still pumping through her body. She'd been walking towards the pub when she saw the three women leaving, Selina in the middle, looking like she could hardly stand without the assistance of the other two.

The women on either side of her looked shifty, and Kate had immediately known something was up. Selina was mumbling something and looking confused. A few moments later one of the women was pulling her watch off her wrist and throwing it into a second handbag she'd been holding. Which Kate belatedly realised was Selina's.

The other woman was kissing Selina, pushing her up

against a wall and distracting her. Kate had seen red and shouted. In hindsight she should have waited until she was closer.

They'd pushed Selina to the ground and ran. Kate was too worried about Selina to go chasing after belongings. She couldn't just leave the older woman on the ground, especially as she didn't know if there were more muggers hanging around the area.

Selina rubbed her arms. Goose-bumped flesh started to appear below her capped sleeves, and Kate realised she didn't have a jacket. She knew Selina favoured designer clothing and assumed the thieves had taken that as well.

"Kate," Selina mumbled.

She didn't seem to be asking her anything, just saying her name as if reminding herself.

Kate removed her own coat and draped it around Selina who was now shivering. "We need to get you home," she said.

She held out her hands and waited for Selina to grab hold. When she did, she pulled Selina to her feet and held her steady while she wobbled a little on her heels. It was then she realised that Selina didn't have her keys. She was wearing a work skirt with no pockets and a short-sleeved top. With no bag and no jacket, there were no keys, no phone, no money. Nothing.

"Um. Let's go back to mine."

Selina didn't say anything. She just looked at Kate with dull eyes, waiting to be told what to do next.

"Can you walk?" Kate asked.

She looped her arm through Selina's and gestured

towards the main road on the other side of the pub, where she knew there would be taxis waiting.

Selina didn't answer but made an effort to put one foot in front of the other.

Kate kept a firm hold of her arm and guided them to the main road. She was furious that someone would take advantage of Selina, and terrified of what might have happened if they hadn't been stopped. On top of that, she was confused. She still had no idea why Selina had disappeared for the day, what caused her to sign her divorce papers, or why she was attempting to consume all of the alcohol in Parbrook.

She saw a taxi driver and raised her hand to flag him down. He pulled the car a little closer and got out and opened the back door for them. Kate gave him a look which clearly told him not to make any comments about what he was seeing. The last thing she needed was a cheeky cab driver thinking he was amusing.

She got Selina in the car and closed the door. She rushed around to the other side, telling the cabbie her address as she did.

The moment they started moving, Selina started to fall asleep. Kate didn't know if that was a good idea or not, but judging from how Selina slumped in the seat, she doubted that she would have been able to keep her awake anyway.

Kate took Selina's hand and kept a loose hold on it.

What-ifs and worst-case scenarios whizzed through her mind. She had to actively silence them to prevent an all-out panic from consuming her.

She wanted to know what had happened, but knew Selina was in no state to answer questions. They sat in silence, Selina half asleep and Kate building a to-do list. It was the only way she could keep herself from spiralling: focus on what she could control and put a plan into place to ensure Selina was safe and comfortable.

The journey was quickly over. Kate softly shook Selina awake and apologetically informed her that they needed to get out of the car.

They navigated the communal entrance to Kate's building, went up a few steps, took the elevator, and finally found themselves at the front door to Kate's apartment.

Selina leaned against the wall while Kate dug her keys out of her bag. She tried to remember what state she'd left her home in that morning. She glanced at Selina who was almost sleeping standing up and decided it wouldn't matter.

"Did they put anything in your drink?" Kate asked.

Selina frowned.

Kate bit her lip. She turned and unlocked the door. The two women were clearly interested in robbing Selina, and seeing as Selina had already been drinking, it wouldn't take much more to make her completely intoxicated. They didn't *need* to drug her, but Kate still worried that they had.

She opened the door and helped Selina over the threshold. Selina looked completely exhausted. Kate needed to get her in bed to let her sleep off the effects.

"Come on, through here." She closed the front door and helped Selina towards her bedroom.

She turned on the lights, and Selina grimaced.

"Sorry, we'll get you in bed, and then you can sleep,"

Kate said. She turned off the lights again. The dim glow from outside would have to be enough.

She helped Selina sit on the edge of the bed and only then realised that she would need to help her get undressed. She took a deep breath.

You can do this, she told herself.

She bent down, took Selina's heels off, and placed them neatly in front of the wardrobe, out of the way in case Selina got out of bed in the night.

"I need you to help me with your blouse and your skirt," Kate said, hoping her embarrassment wasn't clear to Selina.

Selina stuck out her bottom lip and looked down at the buttons of her blouse thoughtfully.

Kate reached up and took Selina's hands and placed them on the lowest button, hoping that giving her a clue would help start the process.

She looked down at Selina's tight skirt and knew it would be uncomfortable to sleep in.

"Damn you having to look so good all the time," Kate mumbled.

She leaned forward and found a concealed zip at the back of the skirt.

"Stand up for a second," she ordered. She needed to be no-nonsense about this. Get it done. Get Selina to bed and escape as quickly as possible.

Selina wobbled a little as she stood up. Kate quickly lowered the zip and pushed the skirt down long, toned legs.

"Okay, sit down."

Selina obeyed, her hands still working on the same

button. Kate determinedly looked at nothing but the button and took over the task. She quickly undid every button and averted her eyes again as she removed the blouse.

Her periphery vision told her that Selina was now only wearing her bra and panties. Kate was happy to leave it there and let the woman sleep. She gestured for Selina to get into bed.

As soon as Selina was down, she went to the kitchen and got a glass of water and an empty cleaning bucket. In the bedroom, she put the glass on the bedside table and the bucket on the floor. Just in case.

"Sweet dreams," she whispered to the already sleeping woman.

———

Kate looked down at her notepad. After she'd put Selina to bed, she'd jotted down some things she needed to do. She'd called the police and filed a report, told Selina's building that her keys had been stolen, called the pub and asked if anyone had seen anything.

She needed to call Selina's bank, but she had no idea who Selina banked with. But she knew someone who would know: Carrie.

She didn't want to worry Carrie or spill Selina's escapades to her ex. Selina hadn't specifically told her not to tell anyone, but she equally couldn't imagine that a fully sober Selina would be all that happy for the details to be known.

Kate knew she didn't have a choice, though. She

needed to call the bank as soon as possible, before the thieves could make outlandish purchases with Selina's cards.

She dialled Carrie and hoped she was doing the right thing. She sighed as the phone rang. It was turning into a long night.

29

The Morning After

SELINA WOKE WITH A JOLT. HER BRAIN WAS TELLING her there was danger nearby, and she tried to figure out why that was. It was difficult to ascertain, though, seeing as her head was thundering with a headache that almost had her in tears.

She took a very slow, very long breath. And then another. The pain in her head began to subside.

Calm down, she ordered herself. She kept panic at bay but knew something was wrong. She needed to remain calm enough to figure out what it was.

When she was able to take in her surroundings, she welcomed the warm, soft feel of being in bed and wondered if a dream had awoken her. She looked up at the ceiling.

A very unfamiliar ceiling.

Her hand was gripping a duvet that most definitely wasn't hers.

She sat up quickly and immediately regretted it. Her

hand went to her forehead, and she cried out in pain. She took a few more deep breaths and tried to remember what had happened the night before. Everything was coming up blank.

Where the hell am I? she wondered.

Her gaze caught a note propped up between a glass of water and a stack of books. She snatched it and squinted at the text, desperate for answers. She skipped to the bottom of the note and saw Kate's name.

She sagged in relief. Someone she trusted. Even if she had no clue why Kate was leaving her notes. She looked around the sparsely furnished bedroom and wondered if she were in Kate's room. She imagined she must be.

She looked at the letter again. She had to read it twice to take it all in. She'd been drunk, gotten herself mugged, had lost her phone, her keys, and her bag.

"Eventful evening," she murmured.

Kate continued that her clothes were folded on top of the chest of drawers. She added that she'd contacted the bank, her doorman, and the police.

Selina stopped reading and let out a sigh. Her head was pounding, alcohol-induced she presumed. She didn't have any memories of what Kate's letter described, but she already felt mortified.

The final paragraph was Kate explaining that she had to go to work and that Selina was welcome to stay as long as she liked.

Selina lay back down on the bed and tried to recall any details from the night before. Or, in fact, from the day before. Everything came up blank.

Somehow, she'd gotten herself into a dicey situation and Kate had managed to save her. She shivered at what might have happened.

How could you be so stupid? she berated herself.

She reached out her hand for her phone, belatedly realising that it was gone.

She sat up and looked around, eventually spotting an alarm clock which told her it was approaching midday.

Lunchtime, not that her stomach was in the mood for food.

She wondered what meetings she had missed before suddenly recalling the reason she had gotten so drunk.

"I quit," she mumbled to herself. "I… I'm unemployed."

Admitting it out loud was a shock to the system. She'd walked out. Left without saying a word. Determined to never return.

Was that yesterday? she wondered, unable to form a timeline in her mind.

She shivered against a chill, which was when she realised she was in her underwear. She closed her eyes and hung her head in shame. She'd gotten drunk, been mugged, needed rescuing, and now apparently also required undressing in order to be put to bed like a child. She didn't know how she would ever be able to apologise enough to Kate.

She slid out of bed and opened the bedroom door.

"Kate?" she called out, just in case she wasn't alone. "Hello?"

There was no reply and she couldn't hear anything, so

she decided it was safe to venture into the hallway. She quickly located the bathroom and used the facilities. As she washed her hands, she saw a new, unopened toothbrush which had clearly been placed on the shelf for her to see. She smiled at the thoughtful gesture. She opened the packaging, applied some toothpaste, and brushed her teeth.

As she brushed, she looked at the small selection of toiletries on display, nothing expensive and nothing extravagant, just the essentials. She wondered if Kate would appreciate a large gift box of gels, lotions, and perfumes as a thank you. Or at least the *start* of a thank you. How did you adequately thank someone for doing what Kate had done for her?

The shower looked inviting, and Selina hesitantly sniff under her arm. She winced; she smelt like a brewery. She put her hand into the small cubicle and turned the shower on.

The water felt good as it flowed through her hair and down her body. She belatedly realised she had no make-up and would have to go out into the world fresh-faced, which she hadn't done for many years.

A woman in her position was expected to look flawless at all times. Not to mention young. Women in Britain weren't supposed to age and so from their early twenties began a system that slowly increased in time and complexity in order to give the impression that time had been stopped and imperfections banished.

Selina tried not to think about it too much. She wasn't exactly vain, but she wasn't entirely comfortable either. Especially considering recent events.

"Drunk," she muttered, shaking her head. "And mugged."

It was a lot to take in. She knew she needed to talk to Kate and hear all the sordid details, but she didn't relish that fact at all.

Selina liked to take the high road; she never wanted anyone to look down on her. That option had gone out the window with whatever had happened the previous day. How would Kate ever respect her after this? How would she even be able to look at herself in the mirror?

Just ignore it, she told herself.

She picked up a bottle of shampoo and washed her hair.

One step at a time, she reminded herself.

———

Selina didn't know how long she showered for. It was enough time to wash her hair twice and scrub every part of her body several times to try to get rid of the smell from the night before. She knew the smell hadn't been that bad. The truth was that she wanted to wash away the embarrassment, if such a thing was even possible.

Eventually the thought of water conservation entered her mind, and she shut the water off. She stepped out of the shower and grabbed two towels from a shelf, wrapping one around her hair and the other around her body.

She opened the bathroom door and started to walk towards the bedroom. At that exact moment, she heard the key in the front door. It opened.

Kate stood in the doorway, staring at Selina wrapped up in small towel, her jaw dropping.

Behind Kate stood Carrie, a knowing smirk on her face.

30

Welcome Home

KATE WAS GLAD THAT CARRIE HAD DECIDED TO accompany her back to the apartment to see if Selina was okay. Her gratitude had kicked into high gear when Carrie had walked past her and ushered Selina into the bedroom while Kate remained rooted to the spot.

It took her a few moments to step into the hallway and close the door behind her. She licked her dry lips.

Kate hated the idea of ogling a person. She'd been so deliberately careful the night before when she'd undressed Selina. The last thing she wanted was to be accused of taking advantage; the very thought made her feel a little sick.

But just now she had openly *stared*. The too-short towel displayed ample cleavage and long, beautiful legs, both still covered in tiny, enticing droplets of water.

The night before she was completely able to control her reaction, but opening the front door to a half-naked Selina had caught her off guard. Her eyes had hungrily soaked up the image.

Thank god for Carrie, she told herself.

She was quite convinced she'd still be stood in the doorway staring if Carrie hadn't been there.

It had been a last-minute thing. Carrie had given Kate the afternoon off and told her to go home and help with Selina if she was there or take a break and relax after an uncomfortable night on the sofa if she wasn't. When a meeting fell through, Carrie decided to come along and check on Selina during her lunch hour. She felt she needed to talk about the signing of the divorce papers, especially as it now seemed they had been signed while Selina was in no state to deal with legal documents.

Kate had been forced to recount the tale, especially after having to call Carrie for the name of the bank. Carrie had seemed devastated, torn between wanting to help and not knowing if she was welcome to. In the end, Kate had encouraged her to come along, and now she was thankful she had.

She realised she was standing motionless again and shook her head. She needed to get it together if she was going to be any help to Selina that afternoon.

Coffee, she decided. All women liked coffee. Kate knew how to make coffee. And it meant she would be doing something rather than repeatedly revisiting the image of Selina's supple chest.

She got three mugs out, happy that she bought the pack of four when she'd started buying belongings for the apartment. It had seemed like a stretch that she'd ever need more than two at the time. Now she realised that had been the old negative Kate thinking, the Kate who always saw a terrible journey back to homelessness in every decision she made. Luckily, that version of herself was presenting itself less and less these days.

She heard the bedroom door open and tried to look busy preparing the drinks.

A moment later Carrie was leaning on the work surface beside her. "She's getting dressed," she said. "She doesn't remember a thing about last night, and she's pretty embarrassed about the whole thing. She seems okay, though."

Kate nodded.

"I see you managed to get your tongue back in your mouth," Carrie continued, the smirk on her face also evident in her tone.

Kate glared at her. "Shh!" She looked towards the door and hoped that Selina hadn't overheard that.

Carrie was grinning, almost shaking as she tried to keep her laughter bottled up. "You should have seen your face," she whispered. "You should ask her out when all this is over."

"Carrie!" Kate whined.

She couldn't believe her *boss* was trying to set her up with her *ex-wife*.

"I'm serious. You like her, and I'm sure she likes you, too. She's a pain in the arse, but I know you can cope with her better than I ever could."

"Now isn't the time," Kate said, hoping to sweep the conversation away.

"If you wait for the time, you'll never do anything. You're obviously into her."

Anything else Carrie was planning to say was cut off by the sound of her phone ringing. She sighed and dug the device out of her pocket and took the call.

Kate could feel her cheeks were on fire and turned back to focus on the drinks. She was measuring out coffee when Carrie put her hand on her arm.

She looked up. Carrie was shaking her head and jerking her head towards the phone.

"Yes, I'll get back to the office as soon as I can. Just tell him I popped out to get a sandwich. I'll be back in a few minutes." She hung up the call. "Max popped in, and I best go and speak with him. I don't think there's much point in me hanging around here."

Kate wanted to ask her to stay. She suddenly didn't feel like she was ready to be around Selina on her own.

But Carrie was already walking into the hallway. "I'll see you tomorrow. Obviously call me if you need anything." She tilted her head back towards the bedroom to call, "Selina, I'm off!"

Kate heard the bedroom door open and the sound of soft footsteps.

"Thank you for checking on me," Selina said.

"Not a problem, I'm glad we talked," Carrie replied. "But I have to get back to work. Let me know your new number and we'll talk."

The front door closed, signalling Carrie's departure.

Kate watched as Selina walked in the kitchen doorway. She was dressed in her clothes from the previous day, except for the heels which dangled loosely from her fingers. Her hair was still damp and swept back behind her ears.

She looked beautifully dishevelled, and Kate couldn't help but stare.

31

An Explanation

Judging by the expression on Kate's face, Selina decided that she looked a mess. Normally, she'd make a snide comment to put her back in her place, but she couldn't do that with Kate, not considering all that she had done for her. No, she had got herself into a mess and she'd just have to deal with a little judgement. Well-deserved judgement at that.

She had never been one to look on the bright side, but if she were to indulge in it then, she'd grudgingly admit that her newfound peace with Carrie was a positive side effect of her terrible evening.

They'd not been in the same room alone for a number of months, but the few minutes in Kate's bedroom had been cathartic. Carrie had admitted she worried about Selina, and in turn she'd admitted that she was grateful that she'd come to check up on her.

It was nice to not feel so completely alone.

Carrie explained that she had signed the divorce papers in a drunken haze at some point. She'd even offered to have them destroyed if that was what Selina wanted, not wanting her mistakes to be held over her throughout the remaining divorce proceedings. She'd appreciated that, but she'd also declined the offer. It was time to move on, and signing papers she knew she should have delivered to Carrie's solicitor many months ago was a promising start.

Of course, Carrie had nearly ruined the peace by making Selina promise to be nice to Kate. She had dramatically rolled her eyes at the order. The truth was, Selina fully intended to throw herself on Kate's mercy and beg forgiveness. If only Kate would listen.

A cup of coffee was thrust into her hand.

"Do you want to sit down?" Kate asked, gesturing to the living room that Selina had yet to explore.

Selina nodded and entered the room. There was a cheap IKEA coffee table, a wooden framed chair, and an old-looking sofa. There were a handful of books lined up on the windowsill, and a floor-standing lamp stood in the corner.

It looked bare and half-lived in, and Selina reminded herself that Kate was so very recently homeless. She couldn't imagine starting over, especially with limited funds.

"It's clean," Kate said, gesturing to the sofa that Selina was hovering next to.

"I didn't doubt it," she said.

She sat down, coffee in her hands and watched as Kate sat in the chair opposite her. She seemed nervous, unable to quite meet Selina's eyes.

"How are you feeling?" Kate asked, seemingly fascinated by the contents of her coffee mug.

"Embarrassed," Selina admitted.

"But okay? I was worried you might have been drugged. I don't think that kind of thing happens in Parbrook, but you seemed more drunk than—"

"I don't believe I was drugged," Selina interrupted. The sooner this portion of the conversation was over, the better, as far as she was concerned. "I was foolish and very lucky you found me. But I'm still not sure how you managed to do that."

"I called you. Don't you remember?" Kate looked up, finally.

"I don't remember anything from last night." Selina sipped her coffee. She wasn't being entirely truthful. She did remember kissing someone. A woman. And she remembered Kate's soft hands cupping her face.

She was fairly sure the two weren't related. Although it wouldn't be a bad thing if they were. She shook her head slightly, wondering where that errant thought had come from and willing it to get back in line.

"I called, and you sounded very drunk," Kate explained. "You told me where you were. But when I turned up, you were being led out of the pub by two women who looked… suspicious."

Selina looked out of the window. Two women sounded familiar to her. Having gaps in her memory was no fun, but she suspected that the memories could be far worse.

"I realised one of them was taking your bag—"

Selina raised one of her hands. "I think I get the picture." She'd been a foolish old woman, played by some con artists right in front of Kate. She felt so ashamed.

Kate nodded. Her brow was furrowed in confusion. "I have to ask, what happened before that? You didn't show at work, and you were really drunk… that's not like you," Kate said softly.

"No, it's not," Selina agreed. "But I suppose that was my reaction to realising I'd been tricked."

"Tricked?"

Selina sighed. There was no way out; she had to explain. Another humiliating blow.

"By Jonathan Addington," she said. "You were right when you said my only focus was getting a seat on the board. I wanted to be on the top floor of that building, and I didn't care what I did to get there. Sadly, that was well known, and I… I missed some obvious signs."

"Like?"

Selina placed her mug on the coffee table. "Like the fact that Jonathan knew he could get me to do the dirty work, raise the company to a level where his father would feel confident to resign, and then fill the board with his golfing buddies, leaving me to wait until 'the right time.'"

"Which would be… never?"

"Most likely." She rubbed her forehead. "I was so laser-focused on the play at hand that I didn't see all the pieces on the board. I knew how to make Addington's a successful and profitable company, and that is what I focused on. I was under the impression that hard work would be rewarded, but I forgot that was the way of Nicholas, not his son. Once Nicholas is out of the way, Jonathan will do whatever he wishes. I'm worth more to him where I am now than I am on the thirteenth floor."

"I am so sorry."

"No, I'm sorry. I acted appallingly. Walking out and getting drunk. I'm lucky I didn't end up…" She trailed off. The variety of places she could have ended up had been cycling through her mind for a while. She felt ashamed and a little frightened. "Thank you."

"It's fine, I'm just glad you're okay." Kate paused and took a sip of her coffee. "Are you okay?"

Selina didn't know if she was okay. She pondered the question for the first time since she'd started to sober up.

Kate had hit the nail on the head when they'd last spoken. Well, the time she could remember that they'd spoken. She had been pig-headed and had burnt every bridge. She had no one. Abi still refused to speak with her. Her marriage was now well and truly over, thanks to the signed papers. Her career was gone, too.

By the time she realised she was crying, Kate was already next to her on the sofa, pulling her into a hug.

She didn't know what was happening. Selina Hale didn't *cry*. And yet suddenly she was.

She shook with emotion as it all came tumbling out of her. Through it all, Kate held her tightly and murmured comforting noises into her hair.

Selina started to relax into the embrace. The feel of strong arms around her was comforting, and things didn't feel quite so terrible for a moment or two. Kate had rescued her, given her a bed for the night, and was now allowing Selina's emotional dam to break.

A small voice told her that she was better than this. How could she cry in front of Kate? The young woman had been through so much more than Selina had. What gave her the right to pour tears in front of her?

You're twice her age, she unhelpfully reminded herself. She was supposed to be the strong one. The one who fixed things. The one who had it all figured out.

And she most certainly shouldn't be the one breathing in Kate's scent and feeling things that she had no right feeling.

"I'm sorry," she whispered as she extracted herself from the hug. She stood up and wiped away her tears. She had to escape; she couldn't spend another minute in the safety of Kate's arms. If she did, then she worried she'd say something she'd regret, something more than thank you. Something that would push Kate away forever. "I should go. I... have to get new keys. Bank cards. I need to... to speak with the police. I'm sorry. Thank you, I really... really can't thank you enough."

She all but stumbled her way to the door and made her exit.

32

History Retold

It took Kate a little longer than she would have liked to grab her bag and chase after Selina. She knew she couldn't have gotten far. After all, she had no money and probably no idea where she was.

When Kate threw herself through the building's front door and onto the street, Selina was standing on the pavement looking a little lost and a little sheepish.

"You're like me," Kate observed.

"I doubt that," Selina said. There was nothing unkind in her tone, and Kate suspected it was supposed to be a compliment.

"No, you are," she continued. "You find it *very* hard to accept help."

Selina's lips slowly curled into a confirmatory smile. "You may be right about that," she admitted. "I'm sorry I ran away like that. I'm a terrible houseguest."

"You are," Kate agreed readily. "You'll also need an Uber to get home. Luckily, I can help you with that." She got her phone out of her pocket and accessed the application.

"The tables have turned," Selina said. "Now I'm relying on you."

"Just call me your guardian angel," Kate joked.

Selina laughed. It was genuine and heartfelt. Kate smiled to see the Selina she recognised.

"I'll gladly thank you a thousand times over. God knows what might have happened to me…" Selina began her earlier thought and trailed off yet again.

"Don't think like that," Kate said softly. She knew all too well how easy it was to become consumed in what-ifs.

Selina didn't reply. Kate looked up from her phone to find that the woman was looking at her thoughtfully.

"Why did you call me?" she asked.

"I was worried about you," Kate replied simply.

Selina looked surprised by that, which was a little heart-breaking. Kate was determined not to pity her. The woman was strong and independent and deserved better than that. She'd suffered a setback, but Kate had no doubt that Selina Hale would be back, tougher than ever, in no time.

Selina didn't seem to know what to say. She stood there silently watching the cars go by.

Kate added Selina's address to her Uber app and requested a pickup. One of the great things about her building was that it was near the central library, which shared office space with the council. That mean that Uber drivers were constantly in the area.

It only took two minutes for a car to pull up. Kate was relieved when it did show, she was eager to get Selina home. The woman looked exhausted and emotionally frazzled.

Kate greeted the driver and opened the door for Selina. Once Selina was inside, Kate walked around the car and got in the other back passenger door.

Selina looked at her in confusion.

"I have the afternoon off," Kate explained as she settled onto the seat. "And I thought you could do with a friend today."

Selina looked deeply touched. Kate worried that more tears would be on the horizon.

"Besides, you must have a wicked hangover," she added in an attempt to lighten the mood.

"There is a brass band practicing in my frontal lobe," Selina agreed. "May I ask what you said to my building management?"

"Just that your keys were stolen." Kate deliberately hadn't given too much information. She knew Selina wouldn't want her doorman knowing the truth.

"Thank you for your discretion."

"Not a problem." Kate fidgeted with her phone, turning it over and over in her hand. "Look, Selina, I'm sorry about what I said that day you came to see Carrie. I was out of order—"

"No. You were right."

"Maybe, but I shouldn't have said those things to you."

Selina shrugged. Kate knew that was Selina's way of saying the conversation was over.

They sat in silence as they made their way to Selina's building. Kate wondered why she was even there. Did Selina want her there? Would she admit it even if she did?

She desperately wished, not for the first time, that Selina wasn't so impossible to read.

They arrived at the building, and Kate followed Selina into the ground floor management office. Everything was laid out ready for her: a new keycard for the communal areas and the spare key to her apartment. A locksmith was booked to come out in the afternoon and replace her locks.

In total, the whole thing took less than two minutes, and Selina didn't even say thank you as they left the office and entered the elevator.

"The joys of a managed building," Kate said as they stepped into the elevator.

"I pay through the nose for that level of service," Selina replied. She turned to look at Kate. "You don't need to waste your afternoon off here."

Kate licked her lips. She needed to play this right. "Do you want company?" she asked.

Selina hesitated a moment, which gave Kate a spark of hope that her presence was perhaps wanted.

"I'll go if you want me to," she continued. "But if you don't want to be alone, I'm happy to stay. I didn't have any plans today."

Selina examined the elevator control panel for a moment before she spoke. "Well, if I'm not keeping you from something important…"

Kate smiled. It was nice to have some confirmation that Selina wanted company. She'd always suspected that there was a softer side to her, buried under the hard exterior. She knew it was a cliché, but clichés existed for a reason.

She wanted to believe that Selina was a kind person somewhere under all the ice. And she knew that part of her reason for wanting to believe that was the fact she'd somehow developed feelings for her. As much as she tried to ignore it, it was becoming impossible to pretend otherwise.

She didn't even know when it happened. At first, she'd thought it was an overwhelming sense of gratitude for Selina's part in helping her rebuild her life. But she could be grateful and not have to endlessly pull her gaze way from Selina's legs.

No, she knew that it was more than that. Kate wasn't someone who mixed up her feelings easily. After a child-hood following all the rules, she'd turned into a pragmatic adult who knew herself inside out.

They entered the apartment, and Selina let out a relieved sigh, clearly glad to be home.

"I better make some calls. Please, make yourself at home."

"You should probably eat something," Kate reminded her.

Selina's hand hovered over her stomach hesitantly, and she looked green at the thought.

"I know you don't feel like it, but you need something. Is there anything you can imagine eating?"

Selina looked almost shy. "Maybe I could try some toast after my calls," she admitted.

"I'll get it for you. Hold on." Kate held up her hand to stop Selina from vanishing into the apartment. She went into the kitchen and got a big glass of water. "Try to drink all of that. You need to drink as much water as possible."

Selina took the water and nodded. "Thank you. I'll do my best. I'll be back as soon as I can."

"No worries. I can entertain myself."

Kate returned to the kitchen while Selina went towards her bedroom. It was obvious that a drunken Selina had at some point returned to the apartment. The formerly immaculate kitchen had cups, glasses, pots, and pans strewn over its counters. The dishwasher was open, and a tea towel was on the floor.

Kate smiled to herself and started cleaning up.

———

Kate had cleaned up, made herself a second cup of coffee, and was flipping through a tediously boring business magazine when Selina finally returned.

Kate looked up, intending to enquire how everything went, but the question became lodged in her throat. Selina was wearing skin-tight leggings and a loose T-shirt.

"Go well?" Kate managed to say. She tore her eyes away and focused on the article about wealth fund management in Japan.

"I suppose. Jonathan didn't seem to notice I'd quit. The police want me to make a statement, which will be humiliating. And I don't have any casual clothes other than what I wear to do yoga." Selina walked over to the coffee machine and poured herself a cup. "It was this or my nightgown."

Kate's brain unhelpfully inserted an image of what she imagined the nightgown would look like. Selina liked the finer things in life, so Kate decided silk. Probably short. Probably—

"I'll need to go shopping," Selina blessedly interrupted Kate's thoughts.

"Go and sit down, I'll get you some toast." Kate slid off the stool and brushed past Selina towards the toaster. She'd set out some plates earlier and was now just waiting for Selina to get back from her calls. She knew that the road to recovery included plenty of water and something to line the stomach.

"You don't need to wait on me, I'll be fine," Selina said.

Kate pointed a finger in Selina's direction. "I'm doing something nice for you. Accept it and go and sit down."

"You're bossy," Selina observed. However, she took her mug and went to sit in the living room.

Kate made toast for the two of them and took two plates into the living room. She was surprised that Selina would eat in there, especially considering the grand dining table that screamed of decadent dinner parties.

Selina thanked her and took a dainty bite of toast. "May I ask you a question?" she asked as she chewed.

"Sure."

"You don't have to answer," Selina added.

Kate's heart sank. Nothing good had ever come from that statement. "Err. Okay. What?"

"How did you end up homeless?" Selina broke eye contact and stared at the crumbs on her plate. She was obviously curious, probably had wanted to ask before, but hadn't dared. Now she'd put the question out there, but looked fearful of how Kate would react.

"It was a variety of reasons," Kate said, diplomatically.

"I see. Of course." Selina took another bite of toast, looking slightly chastised.

Kate bit her lip. She'd never really told anyone the whole story. Not all of it. There had never been anyone willing to listen. Besides, she still felt some unwarranted shame about the series of events. She knew it would be a good idea to speak through what had happened, though. Maybe it would soothe some of the pain.

"My… parents," Kate started. She coughed away the stone in her throat. "They were very conservative and very religious. They had one daughter, and they raised me to be just like them. I didn't question a thing they told me. I went to church, and I never thought for myself."

Selina glanced up, locking eyes with Kate.

"They were best friends with a couple who went to the same church, and that couple had a son. And it was decided that it would be just so nice and perfect all round if he and I were married. So, from as young as I can remember, he was there and he was going to be the person I spent the rest of my life with."

Selina's eyes widened in horror.

"It wasn't like an arranged marriage," Kate clarified. "Just… so damn perfectly convenient for everyone. And I had no idea I could say no. I think at that time I wouldn't have even wanted to have free choice; I wouldn't have known what to do with it. He was the only person my age I ever knew. I spent all my childhood at home, being moulded by my parents or the church. We lived in a tiny village, so the school was in the church."

Kate put her plate on the coffee table, appetite gone.

"We were married when I was sixteen. I didn't know what love was. We both got jobs, he worked for the church, but I worked elsewhere. And I started to hear things outside of the bubble I'd been living in. I started to question things, wonder about things I'd been told. Nothing major at first, just curiosity. I questioned things with my husband, Simon, but he sort of ignored it. Told me I was being silly. The longer I worked outside of my bubble, the more I questioned things. I think Simon felt me slipping away from the church and from him."

Kate chuckled bitterly. She often thought about what happened back then, how she would have dealt with the situation now, but it was foolish to dwell on the past. It couldn't be changed.

"Suddenly, a job came up at my father-in-law's company. They needed me, and it *had* to be me. I didn't question it at the time, but I later realised they were worried about me asking too many questions and becoming a problem."

"They wanted you where they could keep an eye on you," Selina surmised.

"Exactly. And that's when I met Ruby. We worked in different departments, but our work crossed over now and then. Ruby was so much fun, and she was pretty and exotic. I… I fell in love with her. It was a shock because I didn't think I was capable of that. Love. Much less loving a woman. But it hit me like lightning."

She let out a deep sigh.

"We started having an affair. Obviously, we kept it from everyone because we didn't know what we were doing or how serious it was at first. But it started to get serious. We talked about running away together, because I knew my family would disown me, because my husband would… well. Simon had a temper. But I didn't care. It all happened so fast, from meeting her to realising what love was, to understanding I loved her. And she was a *her*."

Kate ran a hand through her hair. Retelling the story was bringing it all back, even though she'd thought about it a hundred times before.

"Ruby refused to run away. She lived with her parents and didn't want to rock the boat. She loved them, and they loved her. She thought she had too much to lose. I think she was convinced that it would all come out and it would be okay. She never quite believed me when I told her how strict my parents were. She'd lived in a home of unconditional love; she couldn't comprehend anything else. Well, we were obviously caught one day."

She stopped speaking. Memories pinged in front of her eyes. She realised her eyes were filling with unshed tears.

"You don't have to—" Selina tried.

"He beat me that night," Kate said. "He'd done it before, but this was… it was worse than before. He kicked me out. I went to a hotel, which in hindsight was so stupid because the money I spent that night would have been a lifeline to me later down the road. I called Ruby and found out she'd been fired, and she refused to speak to me. I realised that she wasn't really in love with me, because when the going got tough, she ran home to her mum and dad. She wanted nothing more to do with me."

She blew out a long breath.

"The next day, I went back to the house, and the locks

had been changed. I went to the office and was told they'd call the police if I tried to go inside. I went to my parents, and they refused to even look at me. I started to realise how serious things were. Everyone was disowning me, and I was left walking around our tiny village with nothing. That's when I saw he had emptied my bank account."

"What?!" Selina cried.

Kate gave a small nod. "He wanted to punish me. I'd done the most terrible thing he could think of, not just because it was an affair. Because it was with a woman."

"That is absolutely…" Selina trailed off. She held up an apologetic hand. "I apologise, do continue."

"All I had was the bag I'd hastily packed the night before. I spent so much time cursing the choices I made when I packed that bag, but I didn't know it would be the last time I'd be in my house, much less the belongings I'd need in order to survive. I should have been better prepared."

"You shouldn't have had to," Selina muttered.

Kate shrugged. "I hung around for a while, hoping it was all a big joke and that they'd let me back into their lives. Let me back into *my* life. I hoped they'd see I hadn't washed, hadn't eaten, and think they'd taught me a lesson. But then my ex threatened to kill me. He came straight up to me on the high street and said that the next time he saw me, he'd kill me where I stood."

She swallowed. Though only a nightmare now, the anger in his eyes as he spat and screamed had lost none of its vividness.

"I got on a train. Didn't have any money so I jumped the barrier and got on the first train that was heading for

London. I thought I'd find a charity or a shelter in London, it being a big city. The conductor saw me and chucked me off the train in Parbrook." Kate gestured with her hands. "So, here I am."

Selina licked her lips and shook her head. She took a couple of deep breaths.

"I am so terribly sorry that happened to you. I… I can't imagine it. I've lived a blessed life to be surrounded by people who accept me for who I am. And while I logically know that many people are condemned for their sexual preferences, I've never experienced it. It's a shock to hear stories like this."

"Yeah, it was a hell of a coming out." Kate chuckled.

Selina didn't laugh. "I'm so sorry, Kate. But thank you for trusting me with your story."

"What about you?" Kate asked quickly. She was never one to let an opportunity go to waste. What's more, she was desperate to remove some of the layers that surrounded Selina like a suit of armour.

"Me?"

"Yes, you. Tell me something about you."

Selina smoothed some crumbs off of her seat. "I'm afraid that would pale into insignificance beside your tale."

"It's not a competition," Kate said. "I just want to get to know you. Please?"

33

A Question of Age

SELINA MENTALLY TOSSED AROUND HER OWN COMING out tale and felt strangely guilty for having had an easy time of things. Kate's story was heartbreaking, and she felt honoured that Kate had shared it with her. Especially considering it sounded like the first time she had ever told it.

"I was blessed," she admitted. "My parents were upper middle-class business executives who let Abi and myself do whatever made us happy. From a very young age I realised that I didn't really see a distinction between boys and girls like others appeared to. I was probably in my mid-twenties when I actually decided that I preferred women to men. Women made me feel more than men did."

She put her plate of half-eaten toast on the coffee table and swiped up her mug of coffee. She cupped it in her hands and curled up comfortably on the sofa.

"Work was my life. I saw my father living an amazing life. He was well-respected and wealthy, and I knew I wanted to follow in his footsteps. Alas, he was an accountant, and I had no head for the academic side of things. Numbers don't bother me, but set exams send my head into a blur. It became pretty obvious that I'd never get to be an accountant like he was, but I knew I could be a member of the board. I could have all the things he had without needing to qualify for something as academically intense as an accountant."

Selina sighed. It was painful to realise that her whole working life had been in pursuit of something that was simply not going to happen.

"I started at the bottom. The post room, in fact," she admitted.

A knowing grin formed on Kate's face.

"And, no, I don't keep Ivor on because of that," she denied the thought before Kate had a chance to say anything.

"You totally do," Kate argued, still grinning. "There's no way you don't know everything that goes on down there. You know everything that happens in that building."

"I thought you wanted to hear about me, not Ivor?" Selina asked, though she couldn't help but smile.

"I'm sorry, go ahead." Kate didn't look apologetic. She looked like someone who had fitted a particularly tricky piece of jigsaw into place and was looking very happy about it.

"My father, well, I'm no spring chicken as I'm sure you can tell. He died ten years ago, and I didn't take it well."

"I'm so sorry," Kate said.

"It is what it is. Time soldiers on," Selina said with a casual shrug. "I buried myself in work. He'd always been the reason I chose the career path I did. In fact, I think I put all of my energy into making him proud and getting that position on the board."

She felt her eyes widen at the admission. She hadn't meant to say that; it had just slipped out of her mouth. She wondered if she had the hangover to blame for her loose lips, but quickly pushed that thought to one side. She knew the reason. It was Kate.

There was something about the younger woman that made her lower her guard. She wasn't sure how she felt about that. She risked a look at Kate, who was looking at her with such unguarded pity that Selina wanted to kick herself. She felt the anger building inside her. All the shame and embarrassment of being found in a drunken heap by this woman was finally finding a voice.

"And now I'm unemployed," she added bitterly. "What a waste of a life. I'm an old woman who spent the last ten years pushing nearly everything to one side in some mind-less pursuit of something that will never happen. Have you ever heard of anything so pathetic?"

"It's not pathetic," Kate argued.

Just then, Selina realised she wasn't interested in getting into a discussion about the matter. Certainly not with Kate who made her feel so… unsettled.

"You know, I think I'd really rather be alone," she announced. She got to her feet. "Thank you for all your help. I really can't tell you how grateful I am, but I just need to be alone."

Hurt faintly traced its way across Kate's face. Selina looked away, not wanting to feel the extra guilt.

"All right. If that's what you want?" Kate asked, as she stood up.

"How old are you?" Selina suddenly demanded.

"Twenty-five."

Selina had known Kate was younger than she was, but the figure still stung. She snorted out a laugh. "Twenty-five. Do you know how old I am?"

Kate's eyes widened in panic. Her mouth opened and closed a few times.

"Go on, take a guess," Selina pressed. Internally she was bracing herself for the worst. She was hungover, angry, and hadn't the tiniest dab of make-up on her face. She knew she looked terrible.

"I… really have no idea," Kate stuttered.

"Fifty-two. I've worked at Addington's for twenty-eight years. I've had my *job* longer than you've been *alive*."

Had. Had her job. Her headache intensified at the thought that she'd thrown it all away.

"Please, I want to be alone," she muttered, rubbing her forehead.

Kate shouldered her bag. "I'll go, but…" She paused and stared at the floor, obviously trying to figure out what to say.

Selina sighed. She didn't care to wait for whatever pithy, life-affirming garbage was about to come out of Kate's mouth. Perhaps it would be some claim that her life wasn't over, some ridiculous notion that things would seem better in the morning. All the claptrap she no doubt regurgitated time after time at her call centre job.

"But?" Selina bit out, using her harshest tone.

Kate looked up. Her eyes shone with anger, which

surprised Selina. It was unusual for anyone to go toe to toe with her.

"I get that you're embarrassed," Kate snapped. "Okay? I get it. You were drunk in a ditch last night. You were mugged, and I know how shitty that feels. But don't get angry at me for when I was fucking born. Yeah, I'm twenty-five, under half your age. So what?"

She tossed her bag onto the chair and took a few steps closer to Selina. "I may not have walked this earth as long as you have, but I've got a lot of miles under my belt. I've experienced a lot of things, highs and lows. And I'm sorry that you've had a shit time. Really, I am. I want to punch Jonathan Addington for conning you, I want to punch those two girls for getting you drunk and taking your stuff."

She took another step closer, right in Selina's personal space. She jabbed a finger into Selina's chest. "But most of all, I want to smack some sense into you. So, you're fifty-two. So what? You're a badass, results-getting, high-achieving operations director that any other business would be lucky to have. You picked Addington's out of the fucking dirt and made it a success. So they don't want you." She shrugged. "Others will. Jonathan Addington doesn't determine your worth, Selina. You do."

She continued to prod Selina in the chest. Selina knew she should take a step back or open her mouth to speak, but she found herself rooted to the spot. Kate was telling her off, and she seemed destined to stand and take it.

"So shut up your whining, go out and there, and get another, better job. And this time you'll know to live your life at the same time. You're not dead, Selina. You're fifty-two. And you know what? You're fucking *stunning*. You've drunk an entire day away, you're hungover, in the middle of some kind of breakdown, wearing your old yoga clothes, and I *still* can't stop looking at you!"

Selina blinked in astonishment. Kate couldn't stop looking at her? Kate had just called her stunning? She wanted to say something, but words weren't forming. Surely, she had misread the young woman's meaning? How could someone as gorgeous as Kate give her a second look?

"I'll leave you to your meltdown," Kate sniffed. She spun around and grabbed her bag. "Maybe call me sometime. It's what friends do, FYI."

Selina watched her leave, still unable to form a sentence in the time it took for Kate to cross the apartment and slam the door behind her.

34

Reality Check

THE INTERCOM BUZZED LOUDLY.

Selina let out a sigh. She picked Missy up off her lap and deposited her on the sofa. She gestured towards the movie that was playing on the television.

"Let me know who the killer is," she muttered.

She entered the hallway, glancing at her reflection as she did. She wasn't impressed with what she saw. She'd gradually been looking more like herself over the last few days, but she didn't feel it yet. She felt rudderless, and with that came a depression she couldn't shake.

She pressed a button on the intercom panel, and the screen sprang to life. There was Carrie with a bottle of wine.

Selina rolled her eyes and put her mouth to the microphone. "Didn't I divorce you?"

"Yes, you did. Thank you for that. Now let me in," Carrie replied.

"Why would I do that?"

"Just buzz me up, Selina."

Selina knew there was no point in arguing. Carrie would stay there for as long as it took and lean on the buzzer to drive her insane if necessary. She knew that from experience.

She pressed the button to allow Carrie entry, opened the front door to the apartment, and walked back to the sofa. She picked Missy up again and plonked her on her lap, softly stroking her head.

A few minutes later she heard Carrie arrive and close the front door behind her.

"Hello, ex-wife," she greeted.

"What do you want?" Selina asked.

She could hear Carrie in the kitchen, presumably getting wine glasses and opening the bottle. She hoped that didn't mean she was staying long. Their new truce might be over as quickly as it had begun.

"To see how you are. You've ignored my texts," Carrie said. "It's been three days since I saw you, and I wanted to make sure you're okay."

"I'm fine. Apart from having my enjoyment of this movie marred by your arrival."

Carrie joined her in the living room. She lowered two wine glasses to the coffee table and looked thoughtfully at the television. "It was the female professor; he claims he did it because he wanted to protect her. They are brother and sister."

"Well, thanks for that," Selina glowered. She picked up the remote control and turned off the television.

Carrie sat down and handed Selina a glass. She begrudgingly took it. It seemed they were talking whether she liked it or not.

"You're ignoring me," Carrie repeated. "After we agreed to be friends."

"I thought we agreed to not be enemies?" Selina asked.

"Same difference."

"Then I must insist we go back to being enemies. I have fifty other movies in my queue. I don't want you ruining them all." Selina sipped the wine, annoyed at how good it was. Carrie had always known how to choose a good vintage.

"I'll ruin each and every one of them unless you start telling me how you are," she promised.

Selina sighed. "I'm fine."

"Okay, great, then I'll be off," Carrie said sarcastically.

Selina took a gulp of wine and knew she was stuck. She didn't want to talk to Carrie, but her ex wasn't going to leave her alone without at least some conversation passing between them.

"I'm processing," she said.

"What are you processing?"

"Everything," she confessed. "Being unemployed, thinking about next steps."

Carrie's eyes bore into her. The silence dragged on until it became too much for Selina to cope with.

"Fine! I'm… struggling with everything. I'm still angry at myself for getting so drunk. And furious that I'm an old drunk woman who was such an obvious mark. Those two young girls knew that I'd be desperate just by looking at me. It's humiliating."

Carrie laughed.

Selina stared at her, dumbstruck. "Are you actually laughing at me right now?"

"Just because you're so dim."

"Excuse me?"

"Selina, they targeted you because you looked *wealthy* and drunk. Not because you were old. They didn't think you were some ancient old biddy, they thought you were rich." Carrie sipped her wine. "By the way, you're the only person who thinks you look old."

Selina considered the point. There was a chance that Carrie was right, that she had been singled out because of her wealth rather than her age. It wasn't something Selina had really taken into consideration until then. She'd assumed it was because she was old, but now she was realising that the whole, sordid experience had caused her to make assumptions based on her most negative image of herself.

"You got drunk. It happens," Carrie said. "Ten years of hard work went down the drain, that would drive many people to an all-day binge. You're not proud of it, but you can get over it."

"Well—" Selina started.

"But there's something more pressing that you need to think about," Carrie interrupted. "You need to ask Kate out."

Selina nearly choked on her wine. Missy ran for the guest room as Selina coughed and tried to get herself under control.

"Excuse me?" she managed to wheeze.

"You're obviously interested in her; she's definitely interested in you. She told you as much, and then you left her hanging!"

"She told you," Selina surmised. She slumped into the sofa cushions, wanting to disappear into them.

"I've had to watch her looking like she had all her birthdays taken away for the last two days. It was only today that I managed to prise it out of her."

Selina rolled her eyes. This was the last thing she wanted to discuss, and certainly something she never wanted to talk about with Carrie. She'd deliberately avoided thinking about that last interaction with Kate, trying to ignore what it might have meant.

"Is this your way of getting back at me for being a terrible partner?" she asked. "Convince me that Kate is interested in me and watch me make a complete fool of myself?"

"You don't need any help from me to make a fool of yourself," Carrie replied.

Selina stood up and went into the kitchen. She searched the cabinets for some peanuts, not really wanting them but needing to be away from Carrie.

"She likes you," Carrie said from the living room.

"So you say." Selina got a bowl from a cupboard and poured some peanuts into it. "She's more than half my age."

"She has a wise head on those young shoulders." Carrie stood up and joined her in the kitchen. She picked a peanut from the bowl and popped it in her mouth.

"Why are you pushing this?" Selina demanded.

Carrie leaned against the work surface. "Why? Because Kate's been into you ever since I first met her. She came racing into your office that day I came to see you, and I thought something was going on then. Since then, I've had my suspicions confirmed."

"She's just grateful for the help I gave her. She was in a bad place, and I helped to get her back on her feet," Selina explained in hopes it would put an end to the conversation.

Carrie chuckled. "Sure, it's gratitude. Absolutely."

Selina narrowed her eyes. "What has she told you?"

"I'm not going to divulge anything that Kate might have told me. I'm just trying to get you to see what's right under your nose. She's into you, and I'm sure you're into her. Or at least you should be. She's smart, funny, gorgeous, and doesn't suffer any of your bullshit. You need to stop wallowing and go and speak to her."

Carrie reached forward to eat another peanut, but Selina held the bowl away from her. "Why are you doing this?" she asked.

Carrie sighed and looked at her ex-wife as if she were the dumbest person on earth.

"Because I love you. We were terrible for each other, but I still love you. I want you to be happy. And I honestly think that you could be happy with Kate. That's all."

Selina slowly lowered the bowl. Carrie seemed sincere in her words, and Selina supposed it could be true. Carrie had nothing to gain by upsetting Kate. In fact, she seemed quite defensive of her young employee.

"Kate told me about the night she was kicked out of Abi's house. How you came and found her and brought her back here—"

"Nothing happened," Selina quickly clarified.

"I know nothing happened." Carrie sighed. "My point

is, you must care about her to have done that. She wasn't your responsibility, and yet you drove around the streets to find her and wouldn't take no for an answer when she initially refused to go with you. Kate didn't tell me everything, but I know enough to know that you were worried about her even then."

Selina ate a couple of peanuts. She didn't want to admit to anything to Carrie, mainly because she hadn't admitted anything to herself yet.

"Maybe I'm wrong," Carrie said. "But I feel I know you pretty well, and I think Kate is the kind of person you'd like to have in your life. She's already told you that she's interested, you just need to take the next step. But, whether you do or don't, please stop ignoring her."

Selina did feel guilty for avoiding Kate over the past few days. She'd thought about getting in touch with her, but every time she tried to send a text, she found herself at a loss for words. No matter how many times she replayed the conversation in her mind, she found a new way to convince herself that Kate didn't mean what she had said in *that* way, or that she'd misspoken somehow.

Maybe she needed to push those doubts out of her head. Maybe she needed to have a little more confidence. Apparently, Kate had been upset at work for the last two days. Selina didn't want Kate to be upset, but she had to admit a little selfish satisfaction that she had that kind of power over her.

"If for some unfathomable reason you're not interested in asking her on a date, please let her down gently," Carrie said. She snagged a handful of peanuts and walked back to the living room. She gulped down the last of her wine and picked up her bag. "I think you two would make a good couple. You balance each other well."

The sincerity was clear. Selina inclined her head, not willing to say anything to ruin the moment.

Carrie saw herself out and Selina leaned on the countertop, wondering what on earth her next move should be.

35

A Knock on the Door

KATE LISTLESSLY TURNED THE PAGE OF HER BOOK. She'd read it before. It hadn't captured her imagination then and it wasn't doing so now. She had intended to go to the library to pick up another selection of books, but she hadn't gotten around to it.

Correction: she'd decided to go home and wallow in self-pity instead.

A quick stop into the newsagent's on the way home to pick up a microwave meal for one and a single bottle of beer had her ready for a night in like the previous two nights. Eating bad food, drinking cheap beer, slumped in her chair to read a book she couldn't focus on.

It was the best way to keep occupied and not reflect on her last conversation with Selina. The one where she'd called her stunning and admitted that she couldn't stop looking at her. And then been completely and utterly ignored.

"Idiot," Kate muttered to herself.

It had slipped out. She'd thought—hoped—that Selina

would reciprocate her feelings. She'd hoped they'd kiss and end up giddily agreeing to dinner and a movie one night soon, but she'd been reading too many stupid romance novels, where one event followed another like clockwork. This was the real world. Sometimes things were said, and the expected reaction just didn't happen.

Which meant that Kate was now devastated and embarrassed. She'd ruined any chance of having a friendship with Selina. She reached her hand down and felt around for the beer bottle. She took a swig and tried to return her attention to her boring book.

Should have gone to the library, she told herself.

A rap on the door sounded. Kate let out a long sigh. Door-to-door salespeople asking about her electricity supplier had been in the building lately. Each time Kate tried to tell them that she didn't have time to look at their paperwork, and every time they said they'd come back later.

She knew she needed to be harsher to get rid of them, but she also knew they probably needed the job. She stood up, placed her book on the chair, and looked down at her pyjamas. They looked clean, if wrinkled.

Another knock.

She decided the salespeople would have to take her as she was. She walked into the hallway and opened the door. She'd expected to see a young guy with a clipboard, a lanyard with an ID card around his neck, wearing a high-visibility vest.

What she got instead was Selina Hale, hair swept back without a strand out of place, make-up immaculate, wearing a black skirt suit and high heels.

"May I come in?" Selina requested without preamble.

Kate stepped back and gestured for her to enter before she even knew what she was doing. Her brain reminded her that the apartment was a mess, she was a mess. The last thing she needed was Selina seeing that.

All the same, Kate closed the front door and followed the older woman into the living room. She leaned on the doorframe and looked at Selina, who stood in the middle of the room and had turned to face her.

"I apologise for my silence," Selina said. "And for coming over unannounced."

She seemed so serious, which made Kate feel horribly nervous. She fully expected Selina to launch into a speech about how they had to agree to ignore whatever had been said before and carry on as if nothing had happened. That wouldn't be the end of the world; at least she'd still have Selina in her life. She could pine from afar; she'd done it before.

"You said some things that I ignored," Selina continued.

"Selina, you don't have to—"

"And then I continued to ignore you for the last couple of days. I apologise for that. I do like you, Kate."

But, Kate thought. She braced herself for all of the excuses Selina was about to list.

"I'd like to ask you out to dinner," Selina said, effectively throwing Kate off balance. "Not that I deserve that after my behaviour, but I'm asking nonetheless."

"D-dinner?" Kate stammered.

"Yes. The evening meal." Selina looked down at the plastic tray that contained Kate's half-eaten microwave meal for one. Kate looked down at it as well, cursing herself as she did. She'd meant to take it to the kitchen but had ended up slumping in her chair with her book. Now Selina was looking at it, and Kate wanted the floor to open up and swallow her whole.

"I…"

"As a date," Selina clarified. "You're not invisible to me, Kate, not by a long shot, but I didn't think you'd ever feel the same way about me. Now I'm thinking there might be a chance. It took me a while to really accept that and see it. So, I'd love to take you to dinner, if you're amenable? Anywhere you like."

"I… that would… yes. Yes, that would be wonderful." Kate grimaced, wishing she didn't sound quite so stupid. She also wished she was showered, in proper clothes, and had cleaned up the apartment.

"Excellent, tomorrow?" Selina looked at the microwavable tray again. "Before malnutrition sets in."

"Hey, that's a perfectly well-balanced meal," Kate argued.

"There she is." Selina smiled. "Fighting back."

Kate smirked and folded her arms. "Oh, you like it when I argue with you, do you?"

"I'm not immune to some banter." Selina shrugged. She looked pleased with herself, and Kate bit her lip to keep from smiling. This was the Selina she knew. "What time do you finish work? I can pick you up."

"Perhaps I'd like to come home and get changed?" she said, happy to push Selina a little more.

Selina licked her lips and grinned. "Very well. What time would you like me to pick you up from *here*?"

"Six?"

"Let's say six-fifteen," Selina replied, obviously having to get the last word in.

"You're impossible," Kate said.

"And you have gravy on your pyjamas," Selina replied as she walked past Kate. "See you tomorrow."

Kate looked down at her top and wondered how she'd managed to miss the stain. She was cursing herself when the front door closed, signalling Selina's departure.

36

No Surprises

KATE STOOD ON HER TIPTOES TO GET A BETTER LOOK at her outfit in the small bathroom mirror. A floor-length mirror was the next thing on her shopping list, and now she was cursing that she hadn't bumped it up in priority.

She hadn't worn a dress in years, but the casual dress had caught her eye a few weeks before. It was a colourful red with a tasteful floral print, wrap style with just enough cleavage and thigh on show to be considered a little cheeky, but still reserved enough for any restaurant.

She'd debated whether or not to buy it for days before finally taking the plunge. It had been her first non-essential purchase since she'd rehomed, and now she was ecstatic that she'd bought it. Her wardrobe was slim pickings, and work required casual clothing. Date clothes weren't something Kate had in abundance.

She jumped up and down a few times to see if she could get high enough to see the lower half of the dress in the tiny mirror. She couldn't.

"Get a bigger mirror, get a bigger mirror," she chanted to herself as she jumped.

The alarm sounded on her mobile phone. She had five minutes before Selina would arrive. Setting an alarm was essential because she knew she'd blitz away any time she had in a flurry of panic.

And who wouldn't? Selina Hale had asked her on a *date*.

Kate still couldn't quite believe it. She knew Carrie had something to do with it. Just a few hours after Kate had finally told her boss what she had said, Selina was at her door.

Kate had demanded Carrie tell her what had happened. She'd refused, just saying that she'd told Selina to wake up and get her head out of her arse. Kate was happy to accept that explanation, not wanting to rock the boat too much. She was on the receiving end of good news, and that was enough for her.

She still didn't know how Selina felt about her, about a possibility of them. She presumed she must have some positive feeling towards the idea, though, or she wouldn't have invited Kate on a date.

I like you, Selina had said.

Butterflies roamed through Kate's stomach.

She looked at her reflection one last time. Her make-up looked as good as she could make it, her hair was kindly behaving for once, falling in not-unflattering curls around her face.

"It'll do," she said.

A knock on the door echoed loudly through the apartment. Kate looked at her watch. She still had two minutes left, but it was just like Selina to be early. At least, she hoped it was Selina. If it was a teenager trying to get her to switch electricity suppliers, then she might just kill them.

She took a couple of deep, calming breaths and then opened the front door. She took a moment to thank her foresight at getting a few gasps of oxygen in before she saw Selina because she looked incredible.

Gone was the business attire, the swept-back hair, and the fearsome make-up. Kate had thought nothing could be sexier than Selina the businesswoman, but she had been wrong. Casual Date Selina was much, much sexier.

She wore an off-the-shoulder navy dress which looked casual yet dressy enough to go anywhere. Her usually stiff hair was slightly mussed, which completely softened her look. Her make-up was lightly applied, showing her age gracefully and with pride. No more covering up, just accenting the beautiful features she naturally had.

Selina's eyes had instantly magnetised to Kate's legs, which Kate realised hadn't been on display for as long as they'd known each other. She slowly moved her gaze up Kate's body.

"Finished gawking?" she asked, ostensibly to pretend she hadn't just been engaged in the same behaviour.

"Like you can talk," Kate replied.

"You have legs," Selina gestured towards them. "Who knew?"

"And you have shoulders." Kate stared at the luscious-looking skin.

"I do." Selina looked at her right shoulder. "I grew them myself. Should we get going?"

Kate snorted a laugh at Selina's deadpan humour. She

grabbed her bag and stepped into the hallway to lock the door behind her. "Where are we going?" she asked. "And don't say it's a surprise. I hate surprises."

"You hate surprises?" Selina asked curiously.

"Yes." Kate put her key in her bag and gestured that they take the stairs.

"What if it was a lovely surprise? Like I was taking you to Bermuda on my private jet? Which I'm not, by the way."

"It's still a surprise. It's not the result of the surprise I don't like, it's the not knowing. While we were driving to get on the private jet which you don't have, I'd be thinking of a hundred negative things that could happen."

Selina was silent for a few moments. "I suppose I can understand that," she finally said. "Fine, no surprises. We're going to the shopping centre."

Kate paused on the steps. Selina walked down a couple more before she stopped and looked back up at her.

"I thought this was a date? If we're going shopping, then I need to get changed." Kate couldn't help but feel angry and confused.

"It's a date, we're eating dinner. I just wanted to give you the choice of where we ate. I'm assuming you've not been out to dinner for a few years, and I imagine that makes you feel a little uncomfortable. Therefore, I'm not the best person to choose where to eat. So, I thought we would go to the shopping centre where all the restaurants are. That way, you can look at the menus, examine the ambience, and pick a place you like." Selina started to look a little uncertain. "Of course, I'll choose a place if you don't like that idea?"

"No! No, that's… that's kinda perfect," Kate admitted.

A smug grin curled Selina's lips.

"Okay, calm down," Kate told her. "You made one good decision. Don't pat yourself on the back too much yet."

Selina laughed heartily at that. "Very well, I'll keep trying, and you tell me when I earn a pat on the back."

Kate nodded, and they continued down the stairs. She kept reminding herself that this was only a first date and that she needed to not put too much pressure on it. But that was hard when she was already so completely enamoured with Selina, despite her sometimes-harsh persona. She'd always assumed there was a warm heart under all the ice, and she felt privileged that she was now the one who was allowed to see it.

37

You're My Type

"ARE YOU SURE THIS IS OKAY?" KATE ASKED, HER EYES peeking nervously over the top of her menu.

"Of course, why wouldn't it be?" Selina frowned.

"It's a chain restaurant," she whispered. She said the word "chain" in much the same way someone might say the word "sewer," presumably thinking Selina was above such things.

Selina looked over her own menu at Kate and smiled. It had taken Kate fifteen minutes to decide on a restaurant. Selina had eaten at most of them multiple times and had no preference at all in where they ate. All she wanted was for Kate to be comfortable.

After she'd gotten together the courage to ask her on a date the night before, she'd spent twenty-four hours fretting about it. Taking the leap and letting her feelings be displayed was terrifying. It was also an eye-opening experience for her.

Securing a date confirmed that Kate was interested in her, something that Selina hadn't truly allowed herself to consider before. Now that she'd passed that first tricky hurdle, she allowed herself to realise how invested she was in the date going well.

"Being a chain presumably means they are doing something right," Selina replied. "Don't worry, I have eaten in chain restaurants before. I've even eaten fast food."

"You've never had McNuggets," Kate said matter-of-factly.

"I did once. In Tenerife, so I'm not sure if that counts."

"You went to McDonald's in Tenerife?" Kate laughed.

"Well, I didn't go there for the McDonald's. But, yes. I was starving, it was the middle of the day, so the locals were snoozing their life away. But I'm more likely to have a burger than chicken when it comes to fast food."

Kate looked pleasantly surprised. "There's a lot I don't know about you, isn't there?"

"Fifty-two years' worth," Selina mumbled, returning her attention to her menu.

Kate's outstretched hand lowered her menu a couple of inches. Selina looked up and met her eyes.

"Hey, I don't care about the age thing," Kate said. "If you do, then you need to tell me now or get over it."

Selina didn't want the date to be over before it began. She knew they needed to have this conversation. Kate was right. They needed to talk about it now and get it out of the way. If they could.

"I'm twice your age." Selina lowered her menu to the table.

Kate put her own menu down. "Okay."

263

"Okay? Is that all you have to say?"

Kate sipped at her drink, a non-alcoholic cocktail which Selina had convinced her to order when her eyes had lit up at the flavour combination and a frown had emerged at the cost.

"I suppose I just don't get your issue with it," Kate explained. "Do you think I'm too young or that you're too old?"

Selina stumbled on that point for a moment. She hadn't really thought about it. She just knew she was more than twice Kate's age, which seemed horrendous, though she couldn't quite pinpoint why.

"I… don't know."

"Do you think I'm immature?" Kate asked.

"No, absolutely not."

"Do you think you're ancient?" A ghost of a grin at the deliberate poke.

"No," Selina said through a smile.

"Are you interested in me?" Kate asked.

Selina swallowed. It was time to go all in and be honest. She'd been holding back, afraid of getting hurt. Now wasn't the time to be afraid. She'd had time to consider her actions and reactions toward Kate over the last six months. She knew the truth, even if she'd only recently admitted them to herself.

"Very," she confessed.

"Do you think that I'm not interested in you? Maybe because of your age?" Kate fished.

Selina's mouth felt suddenly dry, and she reached for her wine glass. Kate had cut right through to the core of her issue, an issue she hadn't even realised herself. But now she knew that was at least one of her concerns about the large age gap between them.

Her delayed response was all Kate needed. She reached over the table and took Selina's free hand in hers, holding it softly and rubbing her thumb across the back of it.

"You're my type," Kate reassured. "I like mature women. I've drooled over them in movies and magazines my whole life, even when I wasn't sure what gay meant. I'm not your typical twenty-five-year-old, I'm more mature in my outlook. If I'm honest with myself, you impressed me right away. Even when I thought you were a bitch, I thought you were a hot bitch."

Selina laughed. "Thank you, I think."

"You're welcome." Kate winked. She took a deep breath before continuing. "The point is, you're insanely attractive to me, Selina Hale. If your only concerns about us are our difference in age and whether or not I'm attracted to you, then you need to put those worries to one side." Kate swallowed and retracted her hand. "That was very difficult for me to confess to, so please don't say anything mean just now."

Selina's heart raced. She hadn't expected Kate to be so honest. So far, their conversation had been light-hearted, but suddenly things had turned very serious. She didn't want to mess things up. The thought of hurting Kate making her feel physically sick.

"I…" She trailed off. Her desire to smooth things out as efficiently as possible had led her to speaking before she found the right words to say. She closed her mouth and took a couple more moments to order her thoughts.

"I never thought of you in that way," Selina admitted. "At first I was too busy getting you out of my car park. After that I just wanted to see you safe. You went from being a problem to being someone I cared about without me really noticing or understanding why. I didn't allow myself to view you as a potential partner as I did believe we were mismatched, mainly because of my age."

She cleared her throat. She wasn't used to explaining herself or placing her heart on her sleeve.

"You're beautiful, Kate. Only a fool wouldn't see that. But beyond that, you're intelligent, kind, generous, and some strange people might even say you're funny."

Kate chuckled, a hint of a blush still on her cheeks from the previous compliments.

"And you don't take any of my nonsense, which I enjoy," Selina admitted. "And… I think I'm out of things to say without resorting to sarcasm," she finished, feeling strangely shy and exposed.

"You did well," Kate said. She picked up her menu. "I'm having pizza."

Selina let out a breath of relief. They'd traversed the awkward part of the evening, and Kate was steering them to safer topics. "I'm having a salad," she said. She picked up her own menu and looked at the offerings.

"A salad?" Kate groaned. "I can't sit here with a greasy pizza if you're going to have a salad."

Selina gestured to her figure. "This demands a salad. At around thirty-five your body will decide to keep fifty percent of the calories you consume and install them in your stomach, thighs, and chin. I recommend you eat the pizza while you can."

Kate grinned. "Will you have a bite of pizza? Just a small one?"

Selina made a show of considering it for a few seconds. In actual fact the idea of a bite of pizza was heavenly. She never ordered one and had no one to steal a mouthful from, so the idea of tasting the deliciously fattening food sent her heart soaring.

"I suppose, if it makes you happy."

"Nice try, I saw your eyes light up like a Christmas tree," Kate said.

Selina gestured to the waiter that they were ready to order, not wanting to give Kate the opportunity to gloat anymore. She had to confess; it was nice to be with someone who could see right through her.

"How's work?" she asked Kate as the waiter took their menus away.

"It's good. Really good. Passed my probation, put a lot of new initiatives in place."

"You enjoy it?"

Kate nodded. "I really do. Thank you for convincing me to take it. Even though it meant I was working for your ex… which must be really weird for you?"

The conversation had quickly pivoted to something Selina didn't want to discuss, but she knew it was best to address the issue.

"A little," she admitted. "But only because I didn't want anything to do with Carrie at the time. I knew it would be a good role for you, a good career move."

Kate leaned a little closer, about to ask a question that had clearly been eating at her for a while. "Why do you talk about Carrie like she's a monster? She's one of the nicest people I know. I don't think she could have kept an act like that going for this long."

Selina rolled her eyes. She took another sip of wine, wishing she had something stronger.

"She is a nice person," she admitted. "It's just a lot easier to talk about your breakup if the person you broke up with is a demon. When you split up with someone, everyone wants to talk about it all the time. People give you advice, recommend strategies, talk about counselling or solicitors depending on their personal preferences. It's all rather exhausting. It makes life a lot easier if you hate the person you've split from."

"Ah."

"Sounds childish, I suppose?"

"Not really," Kate said. "Still, I'm glad you told me to talk to her about the job. It changed my life."

Selina appreciated the neat pivot. "You're welcome. I'm glad things are working out for you."

"They are. It's taken a while, and I still struggle to believe and accept it, but I have my life back. I owe that to you."

"No, you did it all. I just pushed you in the right direction." Selina wasn't about to take credit for all of Kate's hard work. If she had her way and if Kate had been a little easier to handle, she would have given the young woman a large payout to help her rebuild her life. But Kate was too proud for that. She'd worked hard to get to where she was, and she deserved every piece of praise for it.

"You did more than that," Kate said.

"You did all the hard work," Selina argued. "Don't

diminish what you've achieved. You had opportunities handed to you, but you were the one who shaped them and got where you are today."

Kate shrugged half-heartedly. "In council accommodation. I don't even have a full-length mirror."

"Six months ago, you had no job and no home. Today you're a senior operator, earning a salary, paying a subsidised amount to live in council accommodation, and presumably saving towards your own place?"

Kate nodded.

"You've come a long way. You worked hard, and you've gotten back on your feet in an extraordinary way. I'm proud of you. You should be, too."

Kate's eyes widened. "You're proud of me?"

"Extremely," Selina confessed.

Kate smiled. "You have no idea how happy that makes me."

Selina felt a sarcastic comment bubble up her throat. She swallowed it down again. Her reaction to anything too sentimental was to make a joke, often destroying the moment in the process. It was something she needed to work on, something she was willing to work on for Kate.

"I…" Kate closed her eyes tightly for a second. Something deeply troubling seemed to be on her lips and Selina waited as patiently as she could. Her eyes flew open. "I'm still married."

Selina let out a small sigh of relief, having expected something much worse. "I'd assumed as much. Your husband didn't exactly go through usual channels, and the fact you've been living… as you have. Well, I'd put two and two together."

"You're okay with that?"

"I haven't received the official paperwork from the court yet, so technically I'm still married, too." Selina shrugged. "It is what it is. Life is rarely simple. I can help you with the paperwork if you'd like?"

"I've heard that completing paperwork on time isn't a strong suit of yours," Kate quipped.

"It is when I have the right motivation," Selina said, her voice low as her eyes bore into Kate's.

"Do I motivate you?" Kate asked.

"God, yes," Selina whispered.

———

After the meal, Selina hadn't been ready for the evening to end. She didn't want to pressure Kate by inviting her back to hers or requesting an invite to Kate's apartment. She wanted to do this right, to take things slowly and see how they progressed.

Her interest in Kate was quickly ratcheting up. Every drop of information about Kate's past, every new insight into her preferences, every joke spilling from her lips was adding to Selina's fascination.

She'd suggested a walk in the park. It was a warm evening, and she didn't want to say good night just yet. Thankfully, Kate seemed to feel the same way, so they strolled around Parbrook Gardens as the sun beat out its last intense rays.

"Hey, is that the thirteenth floor of Addington's?" Kate asked cheekily, pointing to the tall building across the road.

"Who?" Selina replied.

"Addington's. Some shitty company," Kate explained.

Selina gently nudged her with her shoulder. "Not ringing any bells."

"That's the spirit," Kate said. "Do you know what you'll do next?"

"I have a few ideas. I've had some phone calls now that news of my departure has gotten out. A couple of offers."

"That's great news," Kate enthused.

"I'm not so sure," she admitted.

"No?"

"No. I've come to realise that I might not be the right kind of person for that environment. I'm good at my job, but it consumes me. I feel it might be time for a change, maybe consider consultancy. Do what I'm good at, but not be buried in the firm I'm working for. Have the ability to go home at the end of the day and not worry about what the boss thinks."

"Because you'll be the boss," Kate surmised. "That sounds like a great idea."

"I'm thinking it over. Might be a nice change of pace, give me more time for other things."

"Taking up skydiving, eh?" Kate asked.

"No, something far more thrilling. I've started dating again."

"Sounds intriguing, what's she like?"

Selina chuckled. "She's beautiful, inside and out. Too good for me, but I'm on my best behaviour to try to convince her to give me a chance, despite the obvious flaws in my personality."

"Sounds like you're serious about her," Kate said softly.

"I am." Selina stood in front of her, stopping their meandering around the flowerbeds. "May I kiss you?"

Kate blinked in surprise.

Selina wanted to kick herself. "I'm sorry, it's too soon. Forget I said that."

"No! No, I just… I've never been asked for permission before. It surprised me."

"Consent is important," Selina said.

"Asking for consent is hot as hell," Kate corrected. "And my answer is yes, you may."

Selina took a step closer and softly cupped Kate's cheek. She lowered her lips to Kate's and tenderly placed a kiss on them. It was gentle, a caress of the lips, a promise of more to come but a signal that slow was not only acceptable, also welcomed.

Thoughts of the thirteenth floor were obliterated from her brain. Her single-mindedness had a new goal, to live a happy and fulfilled life. Hopefully, it would be one that included the incredible woman she was lucky enough to have found.

THE END

Patreon

I adore publishing. There's a wonderful thrill that comes from crafting a manuscript and then releasing it to the world. Especially when you are writing woman loving woman characters. I'm blessed to receive messages from readers all over the world who are thrilled to discover characters and scenarios that resemble their lives.

Books are entertaining escapism, but they are also reinforcement that we are not alone in our struggles. I'm passionate about writing books that people can identify with. Books that are accessible to all and show that love—and acceptance—can be found no matter who you are.

I've been lucky enough to have published books that have been best-sellers and even some award-winners. While I'm still quite a new author, I have plans to write many, many more novels. However, writing, editing, and marketing books take up a lot of time… and writing full-time is a treadmill-like existence, especially in a very small niche market like mine.

Don't get me wrong, I feel very grateful and lucky to

be able to live the life I do. But being a full-time author in a small market means never being able to stop and work on developing my writing style, it means rarely having the time or budget to properly market my books, it means immediately picking up the next project the moment the previous has finished.

This is why I have set up a Patreon account. With Patreon, you can donate a small amount each month to enable me to hop off of my treadmill for a while in order to reach my goals. Goals such as exploring better marketing options, developing my writing craft, and investigating writing articles and screenplays.

My Patreon page is a place for exclusive first looks at new works, insight into upcoming projects, Q&A sessions, as well as special gifts and dedications. I'm also pleased to give all of my Patreon subscribers access to **exclusive short stories** which have been written just for patrons. There are tiers to suit all budgets.

My readers are some of the kindest and most supportive people I have met, and I appreciate every book borrow or purchase. With the added support of Patreon, I hope to be able to develop my writing career in order to become a better author as well as level up my marketing strategy to help my books to reach a wider audience.

https://www.patreon.com/aeradley

Reviews

I sincerely hope you enjoyed reading this book.

If you did, I would greatly appreciate a short review on your favourite book website.

Reviews are crucial for any author, and even just a line or two can make a huge difference.

About the Author

Amanda Radley had no desire to be a writer but accidentally became an award-winning, bestselling author.

She gave up a marketing career in order to make stuff up for a living instead. She claims the similarities are startling.

She describes herself as a Wife. Traveller. Tea Drinker. Biscuit Eater. Animal Lover. Master Pragmatist. Procrastinator. Theme Park Fan.

Connect with Amanda
www.amandaradley.com

Also by Amanda Radley

Fitting In

2020 Amazon Kindle Storyteller Finalist

Starting a new job is hard. Especially if you're the boss's daughter

Heather Bailey has been in charge of Silver Arches, the prestigious London shopping centre, for several years. Financial turmoil brings a new investor to secure the future and Heather finds herself playing office politics with the notoriously difficult entrepreneur Leo Flynn. Walking a fine line between standing her ground and being willing to accept change, Heather has her work cut out for her.

When Leo demands that his daughter is found a job at Silver Arches; things become even harder.

Scarlett Flynn has never fit in. Not in the army, not in her father's firm, not even in her own family. So starting work at Silver Arches won't be any different, will it?

A heartwarming exploration of the art of fitting in.

Also by Amanda Radley

Second Chances

Bad childhood memories start to resurface when Hannah Hall's daughter Rosie begins school. To make matters more complicated, Hannah has been steadfastly ignoring the obvious truth that Rosie is intellectually gifted and wise beyond her years.

In the crumbling old school she meets Rosie's new teacher Alice Spencer who has moved from the city to teach in the small coastal town of Fairlight.

Alice immediately sees Rosie's potential and embarks on developing an educational curriculum to suit Rosie's needs, to Hannah's dismay.

Teacher and mother clash over what's best for young Rosie.

Will they be able to compromise? Will Hannah finally open up to someone about her own damaged upbringing?

And will they be able to ignore the sparks that fly whenever they are in the same room?

Also by Amanda Radley

Lost at Sea

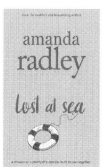

A stowaway. A perceptive captain. Both drawn together.

Annie Peck finds herself in a terrible situation and is literally running for her life. A chance encounter with a surprising lookalike leads her towards a risky solution.

Captain Caroline West knows she is lucky to be one of the few women cruise ship captains in the world. Sadly, not having a standard nine to five job means relationships are nearly impossible and she's all but given up on finding anyone.

Join these two women for an all-expenses-paid cruise of the Mediterranean and find out what happens when an identity thief with a heart of gold meets the rule-abiding woman who could throw her in jail.